The Immortal Marshal

Behind Marshal Fallon lay a string of hell-towns, all roaring, raging and running out of control. That is until one by one, he tamed them with a six-gun and an iron belief in the law he served. Then he came to Freetown, Kansas.

It was filled with wild Texas cowboys, corrupt officials and hellions from all over, who turned the boom town into a hell on earth. Fallon faced his greatest challenge.

But by the time he was through, every shyster, back-shooter and hate-ridden Texan would believe it when the marshal proclaimed, 'I am the law!'

The Immortal Marshal

Ryan Bodie

A Black Horse Western

ROBERT HALE · LONDON

© Ryan Bodie 2003
First published in Great Britain 2003

ISBN 0 7090 7350 X

Robert Hale Limited
Clerkenwell House
Clerkenwell Green
London EC1R 0HT

Typeset by
Derek Doyle & Associates, Liverpool.
Printed and bound in Great Britain by
Antony Rowe Limited, Wiltshire

1

FALLON'S LAW

'Fallon!'

The sudden shout ripped through the midnight quiet of the railroad town like a gunshot. It jolted turnkey Jim Rand awake as he dozed at the jailhouse and sent shivers down the spine of the good Reverend Aimes praying for peace and enlightenment by his bedside on Carney Street. The sound appeared to pick up volume as it invaded the barroom of Diamond's saloon, jerking the lonelies upright to blink expectantly across at the tall figure seated at a rear table with his back to the wall, playing solitaire.

Gil Fallon, marshal of Freetown, didn't stir, didn't lift his eyes from the cards before him.

'I know you're in there, you lawdog butcher!' The slurring Texas twang sounded again, this time louder. 'And b'God iffen you ain't got the sand to come out here and face me man to man – Mr Yankee backshooter – then I'm a-comin' in!'

This was all the cow-licked barkeep needed to hear before hastily reaching down his more expensive bottled stock from the shelves. The clatter he caused mixed jarringly with the scraping of chairs and chink of glassware as pale-faced drinkers and painted percenters moved hurriedly away from the long bar mere moments before someone lean, mean and patently well-primed shouldered his way through the battered swinging doors.

Kit Tonner swayed to a halt beneath the hanging lamps and Diamond's patrons gaped, open-jawed. It was a matter of record that various hellions from the Texas herds had challenged the town's new marshal since he'd pinned on the star three weeks ago. But those bravos had been of a different breed from this waddy. There were gun hellions and hardcases with reps, some hired by the trail bosses specifically for the job of dealing with Texan-hating Kansan towns and the men they hired to protect themselves and their property.

But this Tonner was no gunshark, just a big-mouth punk basking in his brother's glory. Willy Tonner was the genuine article, a mean-eyed gunslinger with a Colt handle notched like a corncob. The big-nosed kid brother was just a lightweight but mean and full of himself, especially when liquored up, like now.

Yet some of Tonner's whiskey-fuelled courage faded visibly when the man with the badge seated alone in back, his pale face shadowed by his flat brimmed black hat, calmly placed one card upon another and still didn't lift his gaze.

'Something on your mind, son?'

Fallon's voice carried weight. It was the sort of voice a man could develop over years of walking the lethal streets of boomtowns similar in every way to Freetown, with only a badge and a gun between himself and the bad ones and the mad ones, as well as troublesome striplings of the buck-toothed Junior Tonner breed.

The herder flushed and his Adam's apple bobbed drily. He was attempting to look mean and dangerous but scarcely fooled anybody. Those closest could see him shaking and noted the light film of nervous sweat sheening his face. They glanced at one another in puzzlement.

Sam Kittleson and his Concho herd had been graze-camped down at Burnt River Valley, south of Black Mesa, waiting to ship north on the new spur line linking Freetown with the main East-West Railroad line at Buffalo Haunch for three days now. During that time the marshal had imposed his authority upon his crews with an iron hand. Just one man alone had forty hell-raising Texas cowboys walking on eggshells, yet here was somebody's kid brother making a risky grandstand play and seemingly for no good reason.

Some found themselves glancing at the batwings in sudden suspicion. Maybe big brother Willy was lurking out there? There was something genuinely scary about Willy Tonner; Freetown had seen enough of that hardnose already to realize that fact of life.

But the kid brother was all alone tonight and, like a reluctant actor shoved out onto the stage, once caught in the glare of the footlights he felt he must perform.

'Ah'm here to let you know that we Texicans is up to here with your roughshoddin' and your biggety Yankee ways, Fallon,' he stated loudly. 'Are you listenin', you back-shootin' son of a bitch?'

That did it.

Fallon set his cards down and rose. To the drinkers, their women and even those opposed to Council's decision to import him, he looked every inch the professional peacemaker as he tugged down his lapels and started towards the trouble.

At well over six feet tall with a long-boned face showing the scars of a dangerous life, the town-tamer moved with an easy wide-shouldered grace, never taking gray eyes from the trail herder's face until he stood before him, dwarfing him with his height and authority.

'What's the game, cowboy?' he demanded. Fallon wasn't angry, just curious, for his lawman's instincts warned there was something wrong with this whole set-up. There'd been trouble between big brother Willy and a local woman the previous night and the marshal had posted the troublemaker beyond the city limits for forty-eight hours as a consequence. Now here was the brother talking big and acting acting out of character. Seemed that any lawman who failed to read something suspicious in a set-up like this was unlikely to make old bones.

'W— what do you mean?' Tonner found himself backing up, hated himself for doing it, couldn't help it. His weak mouth twisted. 'I done told you why I come in from the herd, and you'd better have a nice friendly message for me to take back to the boys tonight, otherwise . . . otherwise . . .'

The man was foundering as Fallon's stare seemed to hold him transfixed. Then someone sniggered. Instantly the barroom began to relax as they realized the troublemaker was going to water. Some were even grinning mockingly and nudging one another, bringing a hot flash of shame to Tonner's bony cheeks.

He swallowed painfully.

How in the name of holy hell had he let himself be conned into this crazy deal anyway?

Fallon was letting the waddy stew in his own sweat a spell. You could hear the quiet, and it seemed to drag on interminably.

Then it came.

At first it sounded like the sudden slow-building shriek of a locomotive whistle cutting through the night air from the distant switching yards. Yet no sooner had that thought registered before chilling reality overtook it. For this was now unmistakably a scream from a human throat, a chilling shriek of either pain or terror that attacked the ear like a bone saw and seemed to tremble the saloon from end to end. A sound to surely scare both man and beast, it seemed to immobilize man and woman, all but one.

The marshal was first out through the batwings. Long-striding out into the cold and deathly moon-light, he glanced left then right before spotting his deputy and the turnkey running swiftly from the jail-house.

'Plains Street, sounds like, Marshal!' shouted young Jim Rand, and the three were cornering out of Longhorn into Plains as a swarm of excited drinkers erupted from the saloon behind to bear a sick-looking Kit Tonner along with them like a fish caught up in the tide as they followed the lawmen towards the sounds of trouble.

The Lady Fox whorehouse, two doors from the saloon, was ablaze with lights and the screaming came from the young woman in the white nightgown who was stumbling across the street. Her hands and bare arms were red with blood and splotches of hot crimson stained her bodice as she reeled from side to side as though drunk or in shock.

The gaunt figure of a tall man in trailrider's denim stood as though frozen in mid-stride between the woman and the house. As her scream abruptly choked off as shock kicked in and shook her head to toe, a fat woman gesticulating wildly from an upper balcony of the cathouse began to shout at the top of her lungs.

'Marshal! It was him who done it! That damned Texan. He cut our Maisie! Lookit! He's still got the razor!'

Fallon's right hand filled with Colt too fast for the eye to follow as the whipsawed figure of Willy Tonner was suddenly galvanized into action. Brandishing his razor and mouthing curses, the Texan managed to keep the wounded woman between himself and the fast-closing men from the jailhouse long enough to reach her without exposing himself. Instantly his free arm whipped around her neck and snapped her head back, affording everybody a sickening glimpse of what had been done to her.

Her left cheek had been opened to the bone.

Maisie Crebb's eyes were wild with pain and terror.

And the blood kept pumping.

Fallon's gesture brought Rand and Ketch to a sliding halt behind him. He still clutched his sixshooter but couldn't fire. Only a fraction of the Texan's face was visible behind the cloud of Maisie's bottle-blonde thatch, but one bulging eye revealed a lot. Plainly Willy Tonner was mad dog loco on liquor or dope, and as he began hauling his hostage backwards towards his horse tied up at the hitch rail, his shout sounded like an animal barking.

'Make one more step and you can feed her head to your dog, Fallon!' he raged. The razor glittered and the onlookers now clearly saw a faint trickle of fresh blood snaking down the white neck where the steel tip touched.

Nobody moved. None dared. Not even Fallon.

'Give yourself up, Tonner,' he ordered. 'You'll get a fair trial if—'

'In this stinkin' carpetbagger town?' the Texan ranted. 'You'd hang me in a minute, and all I done was what the bitch deserved for dumpin' me for a dirty Kansan last night. She said she loved me – didn't you, bitch?'

Fallon threw a sideways stare at Kit Tonner standing in back of them with the crowd from the saloon.

'Is this the caper?' he demanded. 'He wanted to get square with the girl and gave you the job of keeping me occupied? Answer me, damn you, mister!'

'Marshal . . . I swear I never knew he was gonna . . .' Kit Tonner swallowed. He looked sick as he spread his hands and called, 'Willy, better leave her go, man. Judas, did you have to cut her like—?'

'Come untie my cayuse across, you idjut!' big brother bawled back at him. 'I'm gonna run and nobody's gonna stop me. And that means you especial, Fallon. You come one inch nigher and she's meat.'

Kit Tonner stood rooted to the spot, seemingly incapable of movement. The hanging moment seemed to stretch unbearably as an errant wind came snaking down the wide street bringing on its breath the night scents of buffalo grass, the stink of big animals and the gritty waft of the railroad yards to mingle with the evil whiff of fresh blood . . . . Every eye stayed locked upon the marshal. Nobody seemed to know what he would do; none expected what came next. Abruptly, Fallon housed his gun, the brutal black metal glittering as it was swallowed by the leather. He shrugged carelessly and spread his hands.

'All right, hardcase, I know when I'm licked. I'm not risking her life just to collar a piece of dirt like you. In any case, as you say, she most likely asked for it.'

So saying he turned on his heel as though to go.

A mingled gasp of relief and disbelief rose from fifty throats and for the shaved tip of a second the man whose blade was threatening the blue artery pulsing wildly in Maisie Crebbs's throat was equally astonished by the totally unexpected.

As the marshal knew he must be.

As he turned his back fully upon the frozen couple, Fallon palmed his Colt again and pivoted to fire all in the one silken motion. Only Tonner's crazy eyes and forehead were visible above and behind the woman's naked shoulder, but that was enough. The .45 slammed just the once and the Texan was hurled back by a massive force, arms outflung and the bloodied razor spinning high, the crown of his skull just crimson pulp as he crashed onto his back in the street.

Nobody but Fallon seemed capable of speaking or moving in the stunned moments that followed. His actions appeared normal and unhurried as he crossed to the sobbing woman, took her by the arm and led her back toward the bordello.

It was morning.

Turnkey Jim Rand awoke quickly and swung his legs to the floor of his back room at Monroe's Hotel and ran his fingers through his short dark thatch.

There'd been a dream but he didn't want to think about it, for it had to do with death and gunsmoke. Rising, he climbed into his pants and collected his shaving-kit from the bureau.

Early light streamed through the narrow east window and the blacksmith could be heard throwing open the shutters of his shop across the street.

The young turnkey's room at the hotel was virtually identical to the others on the floor. It was some ten feet by eight and furnished with a bed, a wash-stand on which stood a pitcher and bowl, a straight-backed chair. There was a bureau and nails in the wall for hanging extra articles of clothing.

The room had the advantage of overlooking east Longhorn, Freetown's main stem. Of course, now he was working at the law office and therefore identified as part of the town's peacekeeping force, this position could be seen as a disadvantage should Texans start shooting up the town.

Having the herders treat the main street as their private racetrack and shooting-gallery had already happened several times this early season, and had been an instrumental factor in the Citizen's Committee taking the giant step of hiring Gil Fallon to restore law while keeping the cash registers ticking over. Several citizens had died or were injured prior to the day the marshal stepped down off the train from Buffalo Haunch, but not one citizen had lost his life since that momentous day.

Only Texans.

Fallon had been installed in the jailhouse for just three and a half weeks, and Willy Tonner was the third Texan to die, Jim Rand reflected.

If that rate of attrition was maintained Boot Hill would be getting crowded by the end of the summer.

But a turnkey would be a fool to brood on statistics like that so early on a bright, promising day. Wouldn't he?

Damn right!

He worked a cold-water lather into his face and stropped his razor. The face that gazed back at him from the mirror was square-jawed and clean-cut with a short nose, high forehead and wide-spaced brown eyes. A little over average height, Rand was lean of build yet with shoulders and arms strongly developed from his days as a blacksmith's striker at the smithy across the street.

Times like this he still found his change of occupation surprising, and friends were still amazed by the fact that quiet and easy-going Jim Rand could forsake routine days at the forge for the potentially dangerous life of a jailer, particularly with the Texan situation worsening every time the clock ticked.

He'd signed on as turnkey with the council around the same time that Braddock's Citizens' Combine completed construction of the spur line down from Buffalo Haunch. The purpose of this development was to offer the Texans bringing their cattle up over the long trails a shipping point some thirty miles closer than those dotting the main East–West line to the north.

Whenever asked what had prompted his switch, Jim never had a ready answer. All he knew was that there'd been a vacancy when the old turnkey quit and he'd simply felt he wanted to help his hometown through what promised to be the most testing time in its twenty-year history.

Hitting the street with his hat perched on the back of his head, he headed west for the central block. He traded nods with the driver of a flat-bed wagon laden down with lumber for additions to the cattle yards across the tracks. He then passed in turn the newly named Texas Saloon – still closed at eight – the Lone Star Eatery with a thin plume of smoke rising from the kitchen in back, then on past the offices of the

Freetown *Herald* before crossing East Street and making his way along the central block.

He found Deputy Monty Ketch at the pot-belly stove of the law office, boiling up coffee. The two exchanged grunts. Too early for conviviality. Besides, the graying deputy had the same look about his eyes that Rand knew he was likely showing himself. The 'what a night' look common to two men not yet familiar with violent death.

He toted two cups of steaming joe into the cell annex and kicked the bars to wake the prisoner. Kit Tonner sat up sharply and grabbed for the coffee as though his life depended on it.

'What time of the clock is it, turnkey?'

'Gone eight.'

The haggard waddy from Mesquite County gulped his drink and sleeved his mouth. Sleep was fading from his eyes to be replaced by something cold and bitter.

'So . . . my brother's been dead and gone nine hours . . .'

'Reckon.'

'And you're just broken-hearted, ain't you?'

'Don't start, mister. You've got troubles of your own without adding to them. You're charged with being an accessory to a serious crime, y'know. You could fetch five years for your part in last night.' He paused to frown. 'What made your brother act up that way anyway? Hell, Maisie's just a parlor gal. No man with any sense gets all mean and personal over someone who hits the hay with anyone and everyone.'

'You wouldn't understand.'

'Try me.'

Tonner drew sun-bleached eyebrows down tight over mean yellow eyes.

'Even harlots treat us different up here. Like we are nothin' and they're somethin'. When Willy argufied with that slut she told him Texicans is lower'n snake guts.' He looked suddenly proud. 'Ain't no way a proud Texican was gonna take that from no piece of trade.'

'So . . . now he's dead and you're facing serious jail time.' Rand turned to go. 'Well, the marshal will be along soon and you'll find out just what—'

'Marshal? That ain't no marshal you got struttin' round here like he's president or somethin'. Fallon's just a killer with a star. You can hire 'em by the dozen up north. Back-shootin' bastards who figger a piece of tin gives 'em a goddamn licence to kill.'

Rand was half-way out, but the prisoner's parting shot held him momentarily.

'Well, your kind of hero dug his own grave last night, boy turnkey. Willy's got more friends than you've had hot breakfasts. Our uncle Mr Kittleson would have heard about him gettin' murdered by this. He's a mighty big man in the Yellow Sky country and he won't let you jayhawkers get away with doin' his kin thataway. No way!'

The man's face reflected those menacing elements with which Freetown had grown all too familiar since Combine boss Andrew Braddock built his spur line and converted the place into a trail town.

17

Texas defiance.

Texas humiliation.

Texas hate.

Young Rand just shrugged and made his way out to the yard in back. He was grooming his buckskin and the marshal's sorrel some time later when Harry the Bum hung his sorry head over the alley fence.

'Hi there, Jimboy. Say, you got the price of a—'

'Sorry, Harry.'

'Dang nab it, son, a man needs somethin' to settle his nerves after last night. Bet you had a few – uh oh! Looks like your boss man's showed up. I'd better hustle . . . .'

The tall figure of the marshal appeared in the rear doorway. To Rand's eye Fallon looked totally unchanged from yesterday, clean-shaven, immaculately but not showily dressed, bronzed and sober as always.

'You can fetch your prisoner out, Jim.'

'Sure, Marshal.' He emerged from the yard and looped the gate. 'The judge here yet?'

'We won't be needing the judge,' came the enigmatic reply as Fallon turned back inside.

Despite his earlier bravado Tonner was jittery and sweating when marched through to the front office. Fallon stood by his desk while Ketch stared out the window into the street with his unshaven jaw hanging loosely. Rand glimpsed knots of people gathered out front before the marshal captured his attention.

'I'm turning you loose, Tonner,' Fallon said emotionlessly. 'This is valuable space here, too much so to waste on the likes of you. You can get on back to the herd and tell Kittleson I said he's to make other arrangements for his cattle. After what happened last night I won't have him or any of his men set foot in this town again for any reason. Ever. If he defies this edict it will be at his peril. Turnkey, fetch this man his belongings.'

Rand did as instructed. There was a sudden upsurge in the murmur of voices in the street and he was curious to know what was going on. Scarce able to believe his apparent good fortune, Tonner clutched gunbelt, hat and billfold to his bony chest and hurried out onto the porch with the jailhouse staff following.

The sun struck Rand as he propped. Tonner's saddled horse stood before the hitch rack, held by a hostler. A second cow pony was tied up with something swathed in calico lashed across its saddle, something roughly six feet in length, bulky and suspiciously human-sized and shaped.

Tonner took a backward step, all color draining from his face. 'B'God! Is that what I think . . . Is that Willy?'

'Get mounted!'

There was iron in Fallon's tone now. Watched by a score of staring citizens the shaken Texan managed to clamber astride and the hostler handed him the lead of the second horse.

'You . . . you'll pay, Fallon, you . . .'

Fallon descended the plank step and whacked the rump of the dead man's horse hard with the flat of his hand. Both animals jumped away into a startled lope. Dust rose, sluggishly, settled slowly. Within minutes the rider and his grim burden were gone from sight as Freetown slowly turned away to face another day. The clash of couplings from the yards seemed muted in the quiet.

2

I AM THE LAW

'I'm damned if I know what all the fuss is about,' insisted the cattle dealer, pale hands folded comfortably across a well-filled cream waistcoat. 'After all, the fellow mutilated a woman and according to the witnesses would certainly have murdered her had he not been deterred.'

'Deterred?' snapped the most impressive man in the room. Andrew Braddock, Citizens' Combine chairman and Freetown's most successful entrepreneur and businessman, had the floor. 'Killed, don't you mean, Wilson? Shot dead. Blown out of his cowhide boots. Another Texan, and the third to so perish in as many weeks. And him a rider for Kittleson, for God's sake. Kittleson's Concho herd is the biggest we've seen this season and now your precious marshal has placed the entire arrangement for that outfit to ship from Freetown in jeopardy. Can't you see that, you blinkered fool?'

Meetings of Freetown Council were seldom this

heated. Mostly its dozen members gathered here in the courthouse building each Friday to discuss such civic matters as building contracts, land prices, the rapaciousness of the East–West Railroad Company and more recently, the suddenly new concerns of everybody – law, order and Texans.

Today was different. A month earlier following the violent death of the former marshal at the hands of the trail drivers from the south, there had been long and bitter debates devoted to the single burning problem of deciding how best to preserve the peace and protect the citizens without scaring off the trail drivers and their money.

In these wrangles Andrew Braddock had been odd man out insofar as he'd continued to oppose the appointment of a professional town-tamer, a proposition which everyone else enthusiastically supported.

Today most of the council seemed more unified behind Fallon than ever, and the big man was fuming, fearful Kittleson might well drive on north and ship from there.

But today there were a couple of waverers in the council ranks, plus a possible Braddock ally in the town's gunsmith, who now timidly voiced the opinion that perhaps the marshal might have approached the situation at the Lady Fox in a 'less confrontational' manner.

'Oh sure.' The burly boss of the emporium was sarcastic in every syllable. 'You got a cowboy high on loco weed with a razor on a woman he's threatenin' to finish off, and you're lookin' for a man to handle a situation like that with kid gloves? Don't be a damn fool, man!'

'Gentlemen, gentlemen!' the portly treasurer interjected, but was undercut by a bored drawl from the shadows over by the west windows.

'Do you mean to just let these geezers talk this thing to death when you know you're right and they're all-the-way wrong, Dad?' The slim figure of a young man rose from a deep chair and slanted sunlight struck the pale, petulant face of Braddock's son. The boy sauntered around the outsized oak table to rest folded arms on the back of his father's chair. 'You're all skirting round the goddamn issue here – gentlemen. Right from the start Freetown knew hiring Fallon was a mistake, and he proves it every time he blows somebody to hell instead of—'

His words faded at the sound of steps on the stairs. Moments later Fallon himself entered the big room, long arms swinging easily, his carriage somewhere between proud and arrogant. For a brief moment piercing gray eyes met each man's gaze in turn before settling upon the Braddocks. The father's features were now schooled to blankness but the boy attempted to trade stares with the marshal until he flushed and looked away.

'You were saying, gentlemen?' Fallon removed his hat and took a chair opposite Braddock. The man who bossed the Combine and sought to rule the council was suddenly a picture of affability as he smiled across at him. Braddock was a hard man to disadvantage or intimidate. By anyone.

'You're looking remarkably robust this morning, if

I may say so, Marshal,' he said blandly, producing a cigar. 'Gentlemen, aren't you impressed with Mr Fallon's poise – in light of last night's events, that is?'

You could hear the sudden quiet.

To most of the men present, be they banker, stage boss or merchant, the marshal was still seen as a larger-than-life product of the hell towns and the Texan 'invasions'. The majority quite liked Fallon, and he them, or so they believed. With a man like this it was hard to tell precisely if he was thinking of inviting you to supper, or measuring you up for a coffin. But virtually all were impressed with both his handling of the job and the surprisingly modest stipend he'd signed on for.

But the death toll was something else.

True, innocent Kansans had been killed on the streets of Freetown earlier in the season. Yet last night's violence lifted the lawman's tally to three in just over three weeks, and that set the price of peace at high.

Some here had been on Plains Street when Willy Tonner ran amok with his razor, and none was likely to forget the spectacle of a man with the top of his skull blown off by just one shot from Fallon's gun.

The meeting had been readying to debate this incident at length when the marshal showed up. Now most felt tongue-tied, but not all.

'Well, what's holding you, Dad?' Kyle Braddock demanded, flinging himself into a chair with one leg hooked over the armrest. 'Why don't you ask him if it's true that he's ordered Kittleson to take his herd some-place else, and if so, what the hell does he mean by it?'

'You have objections on that matter?' Fallon asked.

Braddock shot his son a warning look then turned the full glare of his smile upon Fallon.

'The young are so blunt – God bless them. But in answer to your question ... yes, we are deeply concerned.' He spread his hands. 'I'm personally of the opinion that you had no option but to shoot that troublemaker, but is it wise to throw the baby out with the bath-water? Did you really order the Concho herd to move on? The largest herd we've seen this season?'

'Kittleson is a North-hater,' Fallon replied, rising. 'He's an enemy of Reconstruction and was directly responsible for the treeing of the rail town of Sparta last season in which a close friend of mine, the town sheriff, was lynched.'

He fitted his hat to his head and went to the arched doorway.

'The man I shot last night was Kittleson's nephew and a known shootist down South. Kittleson didn't bring Tonner and his brother along for any purpose other than to boost his gun strength and have them on hand to turn them loose upon law-abiding citizens.'

He touched hatbrim. 'My order stands,' he said with an air of finality. A deliberate pause, then, staring directly at Braddock, added, 'Just remember, I am the law.'

Braddock made to retort, then covered his mouth. Fallon's stare finally intimidated him.

Next moment the marshal was gone, and everyone began talking at once, with one exception. Braddock was thinking hard on the marshal's parting shot. *I am the law.* That simply was not so, as he saw it. His law was something that a rich man employed as a tool at times when it suited and disregarded totally at other times.

He nodded.

They must come to a more complete understanding on what the marshal's position entailed. Simply clarify a few vital points with the fellow. He was certain they could make him see reason. Strict enforcement of the peace – but not so tough on future paying customers that they might be scared away.

Simple, surely.

'You're a crazy kid, Jim. You know that, don't you?'

'How so, Buck?'

'Well, just lookit you. Suckin' on ten-cents beers when you could be settin' here slurpin' up Kentucky-sippin' whiskey by the gallon.'

'Don't start, Buck.'

'But, kid, I gotta.' Town blacksmith Buck Wells leaned muscular arms upon the three-legged table by the long bar at the Lucky Cuss. 'Look, your job's still open. I've had three different jokers strikin' for me since you up and went and not one measured up. None of 'em could hold a candle to you, Jimbo. So I'll tell you what I'll do. Ten dollars a week more than you were gettin' and—'

'Forget it, man. C'mon, drink it down and I'll buy you another. Beer that is . . . can't afford whiskey.'

It was the following night and things had returned

to something like normal, or at least such was the case at the Lucky Cuss. Earlier the talk had all been on the shoot-out and Fallon's posting of the Concho herd. But there was just so much to be said on either topic, and soon the regular Friday night bunch of friends, too young to be married and too old to hang around on street corners whistling at girls, convened at the Cuss to sink a few and unwind from the week behind.

Togged out in a freshly laundered denim shirt and his best Levis, Jim Rand was keen to invest a couple of dollars on the roulette wheel which clattered and clicked invitingly nearby. But while Red, Hogue and Clarry were also eager to take a flutter at the odds, the blacksmith still wanted to talk business.

'Damnit, boy, you always were a stubborn cuss. But I never calculated you dumb until recent.'

'You're cute too, Buck.'

'No, blame it, I'm serious. Like, when I say dumb . . . you know I never could figure why you gave up a something you liked with a real future to take up that lousy job at the jailhouse for longer hours and less dough. Why don't you explain that to me. I reckon we'd all like to know.'

Rand glanced at his friends. They were certainly curious. He shrugged and took a pull of his drink.

'Simple,' he said quietly. 'Sure, I was happy at the smithy, but when the turnkey job came up, why, I just felt like I was looking at the chance to do something important is all.'

'You think swampin' up drunks' puke and

groomin' the law horses is important, huh?' the blacksmith said sharply. 'So, you quit your good job, you lose a girlfriend who figured you'd own your own smithy one day, you have to quit your roomer and move into that fleabag hotel – and you call that progress?' He turned his head. 'Oh oh, here comes one of your bosses. Lookin' for you, I'll wager.'

He was right. Deputy Monty Ketch had come to tell him the marshal wanted him at the jailhouse. Jim wasn't sorry to be leaving. It was usually relaxed at the Lucky Cuss but it wasn't proving out quite that way tonight.

A silver moon blazed down over the half-asleep town as the two men quit the saloon.

Times like this, when all was quiet he felt an intense sense of belonging with this place which had been his home for most of Freetown's twenty-year existence. Cholera had carried off both parents while he was still at school but he'd been able to get a job here and hadn't missed a meal yet.

He liked the way the town had developed and was still open-minded as to whether the Combine's campaign to attract the cattle drives would prove to its detriment – incidents like last night's notwithstanding.

He breathed in deeply as he rounded the corner in to Longhorn, noting casually that the For Sale banner was still slung across the façade of the temporarily unoccupied Plains City Hotel and Dining-Rooms. He also noted that Chicken Pickles had finally given his windows a good scrub so that now his customers could actually get to see the books, artworks and gewgaws he had on display.

He even liked the way the squat, flat-roofed jail and law-office complex looked with its porch lights on and a drift of smoke from the pot-belly feathering the night air. Solid, he thought. Reassuring.

It turned out Fallon did have a job for him as Buck had predicted.

The wind which had been strengthening ever since they left town was now blowing in their teeth as the two horsemen rode out from behind the shelter of Black Mesa to begin the climb up the north flanks of Kiowa Bluff.

It was three in the morning and cold as charity as Jim Rand and Monty Ketch paused briefly to draw on their weather-coats. Naturally the deputy was complaining about the wind and the cold as well as questioning the marshal's wisdom in sending them out into the 'tall and uncut' in the middle of the night, when they could just as easily have left it until morning.

Jim didn't argue, didn't agree either. For Fallon had his reasons, he knew. He simply needed to know if the Concho herd had moved on, as ordered. But if the Texans were defying orders and were still camped down in Burnt River Valley, then this visit could prove dangerous, so Fallon had obviously decided it would be safer for them to make the journey by night. That was how pros figured things out.

They reached the steep section of the trail where bluffs rose suddenly and sharply as though to protect the valley beyond from the northers that could come screaming down out of Colorado and Kansas at just about any time of the year.

Cattle-smell was strong in the air as they topped out a sycamore saddle where they drew rein to spell the horses. Kittleson's exhausted herd had been spelling up from long weeks on the trail in the valley, waiting for a stock train to reach Freetown. Had the moon survived this late, the herd would now be visible from up here. Unless of course it had already crossed over Crooked Creek to push on north-west for the Winslow shipping-yards as instructed.

The deputy lighted a smoke and coughed.

The starlight was dim but strong enough for Rand to see a bird get blown out of a cottonwood nearby, fight its way back then settle on a branch with a firmer grip.

'Don't see any camp-fires,' Ketch commented, the wind snatching the words from his lips.

'They're gone, is why.'

'Huh? How the heck do you know that?'

'No sound,' Jim replied. He sounded sure as he cocked his head. 'A sleeping herd's never that quiet, not a thousand-head one, leastwise.'

'Does that mean we can head back?'

Jim was growing accustomed to the older man deferring to him at times, yet still found it curious. He was about to reply, reaching up left-handed to tug his hat on tighter, when a hot breath of air fingered the side of his face and tugged at his shirt collar.

In the same instant there was a sibilant sound barely audible above the boisterous wind, a hissing, rushing whisper that was the way a ghost might speak, if it had a tongue.

The shaved tip of a second later came the much louder sound of something small and solid slamming into a slab of sandstone behind.

Then at long last – or so it seemed to Jim Rand – the guttural roar of a carbine, snarling and belligerent in the blowing night from somewhere higher up.

Reacting without even thinking, he hurled himself sideways from the saddle to crash headlong into a patch of Kiowa Bluff grass, tasted bluff dirt and spat out a curse the bluff might never have heard before as he rolled and fumbled for his old Colt.

It seemed to take him forever to start shooting. He was no gunman but had a good eye. He reckoned he was soon putting his lead exactly where he wanted it, namely into that dark mass of wind-whipped brush that crowned the bluff off to their right.

He kept triggering as the deputy chimed in from where he'd slipped down on the lee side of his rearing mount. Nothing like the coughing roar of a pair of sixshooters blazing away to throw someone off while you were desperately trying to determine who, how many and exactly where . . .

A faint tendril of gunsmoke snaked away from a wind-shaped sandstone knob which bulked off to the lee side of the knob. Rand detected hasty movement and fired fast again as a figure plunged from sight. He squeezed trigger as he lunged upright but the hammer clicked on an empty chamber. Driven by instinct, unaware that he was reacting more like a real lawman than a man who just swept out cells, Jim rushed after his skittish horse and was clawing his way into the leather when the distinct clatter of receding hoofbeats blew down to him on the wind.

That didn't stop him giving chase. His horse was solid and ran with a will, swiftly topping out the crest, Ketch trailing a hundred yards behind. It was all rock beyond the summit and Rand went storming over the bulging hump, then sharply down through a narrow defile that brought him to a wide, sharply angling slope which swept away into a wide-throated arroyo. It echoed to the sound of fading hoofbeats.

'Dry-gulching bastard!' he muttered, eager to give chase but unwilling to risk losing Ketch in the dangerous darkness.

By the time the deputy caught up the night was quiet again but for the wind. Badly shaken and pale in the starlight, Ketch was solid ready to head back the way they'd come, but that didn't suit his companion.

'We came out to do a job,' Jim stated, sleeving remnants of Kiowa Bluff crud from his mouth and spitting.

'But . . . but you said the herd's gone.'

'Saying ain't seeing,' Jim snapped back. 'We gotta be sure. C'mon, let's find some good cover until daybreak.'

First light found them wending their way along the length of the twisting arroyo eventually to make their wary way out into the valley – drowsing and empty of life in the first rays of sun.

The sign revealed where the herd had struck off north-west and forded the low-running creek. As the light strengthened the riders grew aware of something reflecting sunlight about a quarter-mile down-stream.

They rode down to find a fresh grave marked by a white-painted wooden cross fashioned from wagon timbers. Willy Tonner's final resting place was identified by his name burned into the crossbeam with a branding-iron. Below this was tacked a page torn from a Bible with a quotation underlined in red ink.

It read: VENGEANCE IS MINE SAYETH THE LORD.

An additional three angry pen strokes underscored the word 'vengeance'.

3

LADY ON A STAGE

At first nobody up at the northern end of Longhorn seemed to pay any attention to the arrival of the stage from Burkeville.

This was understandable.

Overnight, Deputy Ketch and the turnkey had been shot at out at the bluffs. In addition, it had been confirmed that the Concho herd was now on its way to Winslow, while the anticipated Major Hall's big mob of cattle from the Llano had rumbled into the valley to take its place. There were also reports of a heated clash between the marshal and Andrew Braddock still in progress at the Prairie House at that moment, as the overdue cattle cars from Buffalo Haunch came clattering noisily into the yards. They were drawn by a stubby fifty-ton Titan locomotive whose jubilant whistle had citizens clapping hands over their ears in self-defence.

Stacked up against all this competition for attention it was little wonder that the dust-coated Concord, drawn by four span of leg-weary Clydesdales rumbling across the East Street intersections scarcely raised a glance. But this indifference was due to be short-lived as the rig swung to a halt at the landing at the stage depot and she stepped down.

Freetown was no stranger to attractive women, this even more so the case since the advent of the railroad and the business boom which must erupt just as soon as the Texas herds began arriving at regular intervals.

Virtually every day saw wives arriving from the East to join their menfolk, along with dancers and singers for the saloons, painted pretty girls to work at Maisie's or The Blue Room and stylish older women looking to open businesses and ride to success like everyone else on the back of the longhorn.

Even so, the woman entered in the stage line's register as Miss Rhea Tillingham of Kansas City had already excited the overt interest of the stage's rugged gun-guard, who almost did himself an injury in his haste to get down off his high seat in order to get the door for her, only to be beaten to it by a dude passenger who'd been unsuccessfully attempting to get Rhea Tillingham of Kansas City to respond to his oily overtures all the way from Dunsinane.

Everyone moved back as she stepped down, for although smiling and gracious as she had been throughout the long journey there was something about this striking thirty-something newcomer that both enchanted yet warned off simultaneously. So poised and well-groomed was she, and so obviously expensive her wardrobe and luggage, that a man would need to be supremely self-confident to make an approach in a public place and run the risk of rejection. Better to wait and see how someone else made out with this classy-looking lady before chancing one's arm, maybe.

But the venerable depot-master was adroit at handling all sorts and displayed exactly the right blend of old-world respect and beaming admiration as he waved a callow depot hand aside, picked up her valise and gave a courtly bow from the waist.

'Welcome to our town, Miss Tillingham. Is there any way we can be of assistance?'

'How nice.' Her smile was brilliant. 'Can you recommend a hotel, kind sir?'

The old-timer just knew she'd have a voice like that, warm and sexy. He still remembered sexy, if none too clearly these days.

He snapped his fingers. 'Flinders, escort Miss Tillingham to the Prairie House.' He smiled at the woman. 'Best in town, ma'am.'

'Well, it may not be so for long,' she replied as the boy took charge of her luggage. She swished a stylish scarf over one shoulder. 'I happen to be in the hotel business myself and if I should happen to see something to catch my eye here then the Prairie House may have some serious competition.'

'Oh, I sincerely hope this eventuates, Miss Tillingham,' the depot-master said fervently before making his way back to the office to gulp down a couple of his heart pills, while the woman and the boy stepped down off the landing and headed west along the the main street.

Longhorn Street was impressive by Western standards, boasting several large business houses, five hotels, double that number of saloons and gambling establishments along with various agencies, stores, and offices both large and small. Down at the far end of the street, where it terminated at recently renamed Railroad Avenue, stood the newest and proudest addition to both the street and the town's architectural landscape, the gleaming, metal-roofed sprawl of the train depot.

Porch loafers, shoppers and businessmen leaning in their doorways in shirt-sleeves to catch a little air all watched with sharpened interest as the new arrival strode by in her tailored travelling-suit and high-button boots. And naturally they wondered who she was and what her interest in Freetown might be, and they craned their necks when they saw her and the depot boy pause out front of the Plains City Hotel.

'For sale?' the woman said, scanning the banner draped across the façade.

'Has been for a spell now, ma'am. The folks that leased it up and quit after we had some trouble with the Texans. You know, herders.'

'Yes, I know indeed,' she said acerbically. Rhea stepped back to give herself a better view of the building, then nodded. They walked on to reach the salmon-colored Prairie House Hotel where the tall young man who had been hurrying after them for the last half-block finally caught up just as the newcomer was signing her name in the register.

'Pardon me, ma'am,' he said, tipping his hat. 'Hud Morrow – my dad runs the *Herald*. Mostly I get to meet the stages to see if there's anyone interesting on board but I was a tad late today. But they just told me about you . . . er, Miss Tillingham.'

'Oh?' she said good humoredly, arching a black eyebrow. 'And what makes you think I might make interesting news, young man?'

'Well . . . well I've heard of you, ma'am. You see, Pa makes me keep up with the big-town papers and magazines, and as soon as I heard your name . . .'

'Yes?'

Both young men realized instantly that she wasn't smiling any longer. Judging by the way she tapped one slender foot and clicked long fingernails against the desk register her flashing charm and good humor seemed to have vanished.

'You're not answering, Mr Morrow. What is it about me did you think might captivate your drooling readers?'

Morrow flushed.

'Well, you were a well-known businesswoman in K.C., ma'am, and . . . and . . .'

He ran out of words. This was no way for a smart young newspaper reporter to operate. In the silence, Rhea Tillingham turned her elegant back on both men, snapped her fingers for a porter and was off across the lobby for the stairs with a staccato rap of fashionably high black heels.

'Well, you really fouled that up didn't you, Morrow!' the porter accused. 'I was just startin' to make some time with her. What the hell did you say that got her so hot and bothered, damn you?'

'Hell, you heard. I didn't say much of anything about anything much.'

'She sure enough thought you did.' The porter scratched his thatch as he looked at the stairs. 'Wonder what she's so tetchy about, Hud?'

The reporter looked thoughtful as he leaned an elbow on the counter.

'Well, I'm only guessing, but . . .'

His words faded.

'What? Guessin' about what?'

'Well, as soon as I heard her name at the depot I knew right away why I recognized it.' Morrow looked at the boy soberly. 'That there fine-looking woman was in Adobeville two years back when Marshal Fallon took on those miners from the Purple Hills.'

'So?'

'So – they say they were there together. You know . . . really together. Lovers.'

The eavesdropping desk clerk dropped his pen with a sharp clatter. By sundown Morrow's statement, whether true or otherwise, would have thrust cowboys and killings off the community front page into the background. This had the ring of a story with some genuine get up and go.

Marshal Fallon walked down the dead center of Longhorn Street on the central block, giving way to no man whether he be afoot, mounted or even plying the reins of a lumbering giant of a Conestoga laden to the gunnels with gunpowder.

It was a habit the town-tamer had developed on the sun-blasted streets of Rio Duro and ice-locked Adobeville. It was less a challenge or provocation to the lawless than a simple statement of reality. He was there in full view of friend and enemy alike; he wasn't hiding behind stout walls, a squad of deputies or his authority. This was a dangerous town, he was the front line of law and order and wasn't about to allow anyone to forget it even for a moment.

Bunches of Texans lounged in the shade of porch verandas and in the mouths of the arcades today, for Major Hall's herd from the Llano had been in the loading-yards for two days now and business at bars and tables had been brisk but scarcely troublesome.

Fallon had imposed his authority on the Texans the first morning when he confronted the crews down at the pens and told them what was expected of them. Two waddies had cut loose by midday and by one o'clock were languishing in the cells being attended by the town medico after Fallon had subdued them with his gun-barrels at the Lucky Cuss's main bar following a dust-up there. Since then the Southerners had loaded stock into cars, flirted with the local girls, enjoyed a fine old trail's-end time of it – but no trouble. Trouble was out, or so proclaimed the Kansas marshal – and Major Hall's wild waddies now seemed inclined to take him at his word.

There was a satisfying familiarity about this long street as Gil Fallon walked that hot midday. This was his seventh town, each of which had been different

41

yet oddly similar. Frontier towns suddenly swollen monstrously by gold strikes, railroads or land booms, they erupted like blazing desert flowers to blossom colorfully and violently for their brief time in the sun before dying as swiftly and dramatically as they'd been born.

Occasionally one or two would outlive the boom and continue to prosper, steadily gaining in size and stature, armed by respect for law and faith in the future and not just the quick dollar.

He foresaw a time when all the towns of the West would answer this description and there would be no further need for men like himself, whose primary qualification for their jobs was skill with a Colt .45 and a readiness to use it.

He paused at the Plains Street intersection to light a cheroot. Gray eyes took in everything at a glance before he moved on. If his expression altered any when his gaze flickered over the recently reopened Plains City Hotel it wasn't apparent to the passers-by. And if he'd heard any of whispers of speculation or gossip concerning himself and that establishment's stunning new proprietress, he gave no sign.

Roiling dust and the reek of cattle engulfed him long before he clambered up onto the auctioneer's platform down at the pens to watch lithe Texans loading a car.

'There you go, Mr Fallon!' boomed the red-faced auctioneer, his sweeping gesture encompassing a jostling, horn-tossing sea of red backs and baldy white faces. 'We mighta missed out on the Concho herd but goddamnit, if the Major's mob ain't even

42

higher quality. Say what you like about the Texicans, they know how to grow cows!'

Fallon just nodded. This same man had called for his sacking following the Concho incident. Popularity in his profession was a day-to-day proposition.

He watched the loading for half an hour before jumping lightly to ground and heading for the office, satisfied by what he'd seen and convinced the Hall outfit wasn't going to prove too troublesome.

He found Hall totting up figures with an auctioneer's clerk in the stuffy little office. The spare Texan dismissed his man, greeted Fallon amiably and produced a bottle.

Fallon shook his head. 'Never on duty, Major. Any concerns?'

'Nary a one.' The man poured himself a shot and stoppered the bottle, studying him quizzically. 'All thanks to you, I reckon, Marshal. I've driven up three herds in the past two years but Freetown's the best-run operation I've struck by a Texas mile.'

Fallon didn't respond. He treated flattery and hostility with equal indifference. His rewards for his efforts came when people learned to respect the law and didn't treat it like something to be discarded when it didn't suit.

'And I guess it's also on account I haven't found you to be the two-headed ogre they said you were,' Hall continued, 'that I guess I owe you something.'

'And what might that be, Major?'

'It's about Kittleson.'

'What about him?'

'He's a proud man who knows how to hold a grudge. He hails from Mesquite County where Jefferson Davis is still their president and their reputation is so bad not even the Rangers go there unless they got no choice. Sam's a leading light in a Reb outfit called the Patriots—'

'Get to the point, man.'

'OK. I hear Kittleson is planning to cause trouble on his way back home and I just thought you ought to know.'

'Much obliged.'

The conversation was almost forgotten as the marshal retraced his steps, cutting across a junction in the tracks as a gleaming locomotive with a massive green-and-gold smokestack clattered by emitting a vast cloud of steam and exuding power, a symbol of progress as modern as tomorrow.

As the steam cleared he sighted a familiar figure leading his sorrel saddle horse towards town from the direction of the jailhouse's spelling yards on the southern outskirts.

He called and Jim Rand slowed.

'Howdy, Marshal,' he responded with a grin. 'No trouble down here, is there?'

'A friendly visit for a change, turnkey,' Fallon said, falling in alongside. Then he frowned, staring at Jim's neck. 'You haven't had that shirt mended, I see, son.'

Jim fingered his collar and the hole there which was the exact same circumference as a carbine bullet. 'Not yet,' he conceded.

They covered a half-block in silence before Fallon halted him.

'You could have been killed out at the valley, turnkey.'

'I'm sure glad I wasn't.'

'You know, as you're a turnkey, I don't have any right to assign you risky jobs. But on the other hand I can't guarantee you might not find yourself at risk again in the future, in which case, I suppose the least I can do is instruct you in the rudiments of self-defence. Unless you have some objection, of course?'

'You mean, teach me to handle a sixgun?'

'Meet me at the gulch in back of the funeral home in half an hour.'

'Whatever you say, Marshal.'

Sweat trickled down Jim Rand's face. Drawing a revolver, dry-snapping the hammer, holstering the piece then repeating the process repeatedly was far more strenuous than he'd thought. He'd never had much interest in hand guns but was a crack shot with a rifle, had been since a boy.

Tall and bare-headed and with his coat hanging off a tree nearby, Fallon took Jim's weapon from him and inserted two slugs, snapped the chamber shut.

'Hit the trunk of that tree just above my coat, Mr Rand. If you damage the coat I'll insist on full resti-tution.'

Times it was hard to tell whether Fallon was seri-ous or not.

'Whatever you say, Marshal.'

The gulch rocked to two crashing explosions. The tree remained undamaged as, thankfully, did the tailored jacket.

'Now that was disappointing,' said Fallon. 'Do you know why?'

'Pretty plain, isn't it?'

'Don't get sassy, mister. My cardinal rule where gunplay is concerned is simple, namely, always hit what you aim for. Don't miss. Shoot straight. A fast draw is a mighty big asset, but accuracy is what counts. I've fought for my life more times than I want to remember, but I couldn't count the times some hot-shot has edged me on the draw then missed me by a mile. So, what does all that mean to you, mister?'

'Practice?'

'Got it in one.'

So the session continued, seemingly endlessly from Rand's point of view. Yet he was bolstered by the thought: It can't hurt to know how to handle a .45 properly – even if he had no real expectation of being called upon to use one in a dangerous situation again.

'All right,' Fallon said at length. 'You seem to be mastering the basics. Just two more shots. And tell me – what don't you do?'

'I don't miss.'

'How simple can anything be. OK, take aim, keep steady—'

Fallon's words were cut off by the sudden sound of a slow, ironic handclap coming from the rim of the gulch behind. Both men whirled. Rhea Tillingham, new owner of the Plains City Hotel, stood above them outlined against the dusty sky. Of course she looked striking – Jim Rand had never met a more handsome or stylish woman, although she did tend to intimidate at times. Like now.

'Bravo! Bravo!' Her voice reeked with sarcasm. 'Oh I do so love a man who is true to his craft. So, is this a new phase for you, Marshal? Plucking them from the cradle and teaching them how to kill and be killed? How commendable. Obviously there has to be a limit to how many men you can kill personally, so what a stroke of genius to—'

'I think you've said about enough, Rhea,' Fallon broke in, and it was the first time Jim Rand had seen the man at a disadvantage. 'All right, turnkey, that will do us for today.' He paused and stared directly up at the woman. 'But I expect you to practice, practice, practice. Speed will come later, but I want you to concentrate—'

'Make sure you do as the marshal says, Jim Rand,' Rhea cut in. 'With a little luck you might even get to kill three or four people before some drunken cowboy kills you.'

She whirled to go and Fallon went up that slope of the gulch faster than a gaping Rand would have thought possible. He saw him grab the woman's arm and she tossed her black hair in anger before the rim cut them off from view.

It was a long time before he put on hat and jacket and followed.

4

FALLEN IDOL

'You sure about this, Hud?'

'Course I am, Jim.'

'What makes you so certain?'

'I just saw them with my own eyes.'

'What? Making love . . . ?'

'Don't be loco, man. But I saw what I saw. Maybe you'd better come take a look and draw your own conclusions.'

Jim took his hat down from the jailhouse rack.

'Lead the way.'

It was just after church-time Sunday morning and the day felt fresh and untouched as the two men strode down Longhorn making for the junction with Plains Street.

Sure enough, when they arrived Morrow gestured up at the balcony of Rhea Tillingham's suite, and there they were. The new owner of the hotel resplendent in some kind of highly stylish négligée, sipping coffee at a damask-covered table and smiling at the

49

marshal, puffing a cigar in his shirt-sleeves, seated opposite.

'Well I'll be . . .' Jim breathed. Then he grinned broadly. 'Well, nobody can't say after this that romance doesn't blossom fast in Freetown, for all its drawbacks.'

'Not fast, Jim my boy,' Morrow stated, tapping the side of his nose. 'This didn't just begin. Trust an old newsman, partner. I knew about this when your Miss Tillingham first arrived. She and your new boss were together for six months in Adobeville, and I mean together. I just didn't tell you about it, is all. Not until I was sure.'

'Well, I'm happy for them, damn happy.'

Morrow indicated a pair of plump matrons nearby staring upwards with their spectacles glinting disapprovingly.

'Not for everybody by the looks, Jimbo.'

Jim was smiling broadly. 'No, I guess not . . .'

'A disgrace and an insult to the entire community!' was how Andrew Braddock described what in essence was pretty much an everyday kind of happening in wide-open Freetown. He was addressing a meeting of Council called by himself to discuss the marshal's continuing tenure of office. 'Such blatant disregard of moral values is not to be tolerated, and I declare Fallon unfit to continue and hereby call for the cancellation of his contract.'

But everyone on the Citizen's Committee knew their chairman was talking through his billfold, still smarting because Fallon imposed restrictions where the Texans were concerned that were costing him hard money. Added to this, the rich man's assumption of the high moral ground was laughable; he had all the illicit liaisons money could buy.

Yet Braddock insisted a vote be taken, which was carried the town-tamer's way eleven to one and from that moment the romance ceased to be a topic anyplace except maybe at the Ladies' Day afternoons at the church.

Two days later a small but significant trail crew of fewer than a dozen dusted in from the South, took a week to ship out and blow out, then left amicably without a single incident.

It was a good omen.

None could foresee it at that moment, yet the manner in which that Dallas herd was accepted and its business transacted was destined to set a pattern for Freetown which covered the following six weeks as spring gave over to summer and the trains continued to clatter down empty from the North then groan away laden to the gunnels with prime beef *en route* to meet the needs of a beef-hungry East.

Of course no working trailtown could accommodate thousands of maverick cattle and hundreds of trail-jaded cowpokes without things getting a little out of hand from time to time, and they were busy times at the jailhouse for Jim Rand, especially when Fallon hauled in batches of offenders at five or six at a time.

But the wild times plateaued out overall. There was one accidental killing and enough serious injuries to keep the doc's four-bunk hospital busy.

There were savage hangovers, the occasional attempted riot and any number of cracked skulls courtesy of Fallon's sixgun barrels.

Yet still there were no boil-overs, murders or the molesting of decent citizens, with Fallon on patrol day and night. There was occasional news concerning Kittleson and his Mesquite County crew who had remained up at Winslow, where it was rumored the cattle boss was trying to stir up local support for an enquiry into both the death of the cattleman's nephew Willy Tonner, and Freetown's perceived bias against citizens of the Lone Star State.

Time sped by and Jim Rand shared some fine times with Fallon and Rhea, sometimes riding the rangeland with them in day-long stretches, other times enjoying the hospitality of the hotel where all the girls seemed to have developed at least some kind of crush on their employer's handsome beau.

Still, like Jim Rand, nobody could quite understand the complexities of the relationship. For how could it be love if Rhea was so violently opposed to violence, gun law and professional town-tamers as a class, yet had still apparently come here to set herself up in business just to be with maybe the most famous two-gun lawman in all Kansas?

Unless, of course, this was a strange kind of love they'd never encountered before.

Midnight came and went with a muted chiming of clocks beating onwards to two, then three in this hushed and windless night. The turnkey made his shadowy way by the City Billiards Parlor, Clackett's

Cowboy Store, then on past the bolted and buttressed metal doors of the Union Bank, where a cat with silver eyes watched his passing.

Why couldn't he sleep?

What was the reason he'd tossed restlessly for two hours at Monroe's before finally flinging out of bed, dressing again in the half-dark and taking to the streets?

He paused by the horse trough out front of Diamond's to remove his hat and run fingers through his hair. His eyes were gritty with tiredness and Freetown was quiet as an open grave. No lowing cattle in the yards, no drunken herders preventing them from closing the doors at the Texas Saloon or the Lone Star Eatery. Just a scatter of fitful street-lights and a yellowed sheet of newspaper pushed along by a breeze he couldn't even feel.

He half-grinned when he went to the corner and looked along at the Plains City to see the lobby-lights still burning. Rhea Tillingham would have left them on for the marshal who'd ridden out to Poorville earlier to investigate a disturbance, he knew. For two people who would apparently rather die than even consider the word 'marriage', they were remarkably devoted.

He sobered.

He believed he now had an inkling of how things were between them. She hated what Fallon did for a living; he was dedicated to it with a passion bordering on the obsessive. It was a plain case of opposites attracting. Nothing complicated about that.

Making his way back across the main stem, he

glanced up at darkened windows. Honest men were sleeping peacefully in Freetown tonight, consciences clear. Yet several hours earlier when the marshal had attempted to muster volunteers to accompany him out to Poorville where there had been the possibility of a riot, there hadn't been a single taker.

A funny place, Freetown, he mused. Prosperous now, forward-looking and law-abiding. And as thoroughly gutless as a dressed-out steer.

Or was that being too harsh? Maybe.

He was leaning on the hitch rail before the looming dark bulk of the Rialto Emporium when he felt it.

At first he thought it was a vibration in the air itself, although what could be the cause of it he couldn't figure.

Then he bent his head to stare at the ground beneath his feet. It was coming from the earth, a barely perceptible murmur at first, as though perhaps a silent locomotive was moving ponderously along cold steel tracks and disturbing the earth beneath.

Yet as he bent lower, feeling like a fool all alone out here in the main street, the vibration, though still faint grew steadily stronger and more rhythmical – until he straightened abruptly to stare north-west in the direction of the marshalling yards.

Somewhere out there in the blazing moonlight, horsemen were riding.

He glanced towards the shadowy bulk of the Plains City Hotel for a moment. Too bad the marshal wasn't back yet. Maybe he should raise the alarm? Then he shook his head. No. No need to get twitchy. It wouldn't be the first time herders or railroad labor arrived during the night. He'd go see who it was then decide what to do.

This proved to be a mistake.

His arms were pinned against his body. Hard-boned fists pounded his face and ribs and he was powerless to hit back. Suddenly he was lifted off his feet and backslammed to earth.

They'd come at him in a rush from the unlighted marshalling yards and he hadn't stood a chance. He tried to rise now but someone was standing on his chest.

'Jayhawker bastard!'

'Fallon's lickspittle!'

Then dimly above the rush of blood in his ears, a vaguely familiar twang.

'Howcome a feller of your stripe sucks up after a hog-butcher like Fallon anyways, Rand? He's rich and snooty while you're just the nobody who sweeps out for him. You should be with us Texans, not agin' us, boy!'

'Ah, git outta the away and let me at him,' chimed in another. 'He's got the jailhouse stink and that's all that signifies to me!'

Crash!

Something hard slammed the side of his head as he struggled to one knee. He fell onto his back and tasted blood in his mouth. The boots were going in now and the depot lights dimmed in his vision. Dimly, as he felt himself sinking into unconsciousness, he heard a voice, recognized it and felt a surge of hope. Then he passed out.

'Get away from that man. Now!'

The tall figure had come in on the fifteen-man pack of Texans from the cover of the auctioneer's office. There was barely time for the attackers to back away from Jim Rand's unconscious figure before the marshal was standing directly before them with a yellow-stocked Winchester repeater held slanted across his body at waist level.

A man dressed all in black made a lightning motion towards his gun belt and the Winchester muzzle lifted just one inch.

'Go ahead!' Fallon's voice was iron. 'I'd as soon kill scum like you as jail you any day of the week. Now back up you sons of bitches, and you – yes you, Tonner – come here!'

For the lean-bodied man with the yellow hair and tied-down cutter was indeed Kittleson's nephew and the brother of the late Willy Tonner now resting in the cemetery out past One Tree Hill.

The hardcase hesitated, glancing first at brooding Sam Kittleson, then across at the man in black. Kittleson then nodded to Tonner, who stepped forward confidently.

'What?' he challenged.

The loss of his brother followed by six weeks up in Winslow mixing with embittered Texans had changed and hardened Kit Tonner. He was almost cocky as he hooked thumbs in shell belt and spread dusty range-boots wide.

'What's on your mind, Fallon? Or can I guess? You're about to move us on, right? Dirty, ugly

Texicans clutterin' up your fancy town? Well, think again on account we got you covered on that one. Ain't that right, Unc?'

'Damn right, boy.'

Sam Kittleson stepped forward to meet Fallon's level gray stare, his ugly trailhound at his heels. He reached inside his weather-streaked hip jacket to produce a stiff envelope.

'I went to see the marshal of Winslow to tell him we intended stopping over here to pay our respects to my nephew who you murdered. Told him you were likely to try and move us on. So he looked into it and found what he calls a statute that says it ain't legal to post any American citizen from anyplace except where national security is concerned. You want to look at this here document, man-killer?'

The rancher's voice dripped with venom. Fallon flicked a glance at the man in black then shook his head.

'I don't need to,' he said. 'What Miller says there is so—'

'So you admit you acted illegal in moving us on before?'

'Don't interrupt me again, mister.' Fallon stepped closer. 'You've got twenty-four hours to pay your respects and answer charges of assaulting my turnkey. Then you will leave, statute or no.'

'I'm OK, Marshal,' muttered Rand, who'd come to and hauled himself up against the fence.

'Sure he's OK,' Kittleson said. 'He braced us for no reason and we was entitled to fight back. I've got fourteen witnesses to back that up, jayhawker.'

'Leave it lie, Marshal, ' said Jim, sleeving his face. 'Not worth fussing about.'

'I'll decide on it later.' Fallon moved across to the dark-garbed man with the silver conchos ornamenting gunbelt and hatband. 'Your face looks familiar. What's your name?'

'Why, I'm Quade,' came the soft-voiced reply. 'Emil Quade. Could be you know my name, Marshal?'

Fallon recognized it right enough, as did Jim Rand. It was a name with a sting in the tail. Emil Quade sprang from distant southern regions but his notoriety with the guns had reached Kansas and beyond.

The marshal nodded as though in acknowledgement of an understood truth. A bunch of hard-faced Texas trailsmen, a grieving brother and uncle and a notorious *pistolero* from the plains formed a composite picture to his lawman's eye that was anything but reassuring.

It seemed to the silent men that he was tossing a loop inside his mind, deciding whether to bring this situation to a head here and now or let the rope run loose and see what might develop.

The latter choice won out.

'Very well, do what you've come to do.' He paused there, allowing each sullen rider to feel the weight of his eyes. 'You've still only twenty-four hours.' He nodded eastwards where the thin gray of the false dawn was bleeding into the sky. 'You'll be beyond the town limits this time tomorrow.' He slung the Winchester barrel back over one shoulder, his finger still on the trigger. 'Now, get out of my sight.'

Kittleson took an angry step toward him, but Quade's soft voice held him.

'Easy, boss man,' he said, revealing their exact status. 'It's been a long ride in hard saddles. Let's go find someplace nice and peaceful where we can rest up. Could be a big day afore it's over. What say you, Marshal?'

Fallon didn't answer. He'd said all he had to say. For now.

The Texas killer said, 'Have another shot, boy. Put hair on your chest.'

'Don't mind if I do, Mr Quade,' Kyle Braddock replied with just a slight slur. 'Then maybe you'll tell me that story about your fight with the Mexicans at Casa Robles again, huh?'

Braddock's son was having the time of his life. It had taken him until late afternoon before he could slip away from the family home and make his way to the Lucky Cuss saloon, where the men whose presence was making the whole town jittery had made their base.

He'd never made a smarter decision, he reflected as he sipped sourmash from a glittering glass, amusing himself by reflecting on how much he detested the marshal and what good old boys his Texan buddies were.

It was not a healthy mind but it found stimulation, excitement and a real sense of purpose in the atmosphere permeating this saloon, which seemed to grow more menacing and focused as the long night wore on.

The kid had sensed from the outset that Kittleson and the sinister Quade were hatching something against Fallon. By the time midnight came and went in a blurry alcoholic haze for the wealthiest young man in town the Texans were treating him as an ally and spoke freely before him, adding to his suspicions.

Until Kit Tonner finally glanced up at the brass clock behind the bar and announced: 'It's about come time to do what we came for, I reckon.'

By this Kyle was so worked up, so certain he knew exactly what the bitter-eyed Texan meant, that he flung a ten-dollar bill on the wet bar and shouted: 'A round of your best for all my great Texas buddies, barkeep!'

This covered virtually everybody left beneath the Lucky Cuss's spider-haunted rafters. The locals had left for home long before. But they weren't sleeping. Not tonight.

Tears spilled down her cheeks as she stared down at her hands locked in her lap.

'I knew it would come to this,' she whispered fiercely. 'Sooner or later I knew you'd have to create a truly impossible situation in order that the great Gil Fallon might prove himself one more time against the odds. You don't have to do this.'

'They created the situation and I have to deal with it.'

'Why?'

Fallon placed his hat on his head carefully. The remains of a late-night supper cluttered the small table in the center of the suite. From the street below came the faint murmur of voices.

'Because I am the law,' he said softly, then turned and was gone.

It was an old scene between them being played out yet again. It always ended in misunderstandings and bitter tears. But by the time he was crossing the yard in back of the hotel the marshal had forgotten it.

For the enemy was abroad tonight. He could smell him, and he trailed the scent all the way to the darkened Lone Star Eatery where dark figures stood in a bunch staring off towards the lights of the hotel where they thought him to be. There was a sudden hissed intake of breath as the Texans grew aware of him standing there, so close, so still. So sharp was their shock that at least half their number fell back a pace or two despite all their bravado and whiskey-fuelled hostility.

But Kittleson stood his ground as did Kit Tonner on his left and Emil Quade on the right. The rancher made to speak but Fallon wasn't here to listen.

'I've decided your time is up,' he stated in a clear voice that carried. 'I am therefore bringing your agreed departure time ahead to right now. Go get your horses and get gone. I'll arrest any man left on the street in five minutes' time and he'll be duly charged with unlawful assembly and defiance of official authority. Start moving!'

It was a game of bluff, and Fallon was winning it, when a familiar voice slurred from the far end of the crescent of men facing the saloon.

'Don't back water now, you Texans. He's all piss

and wind, this flash dog. Remember what you came back for. Kit – you remember, don't you?'

The voice of a drunken young local proved to be the catalyst that triggered Kittleson's anger.

'You fraud, Fallon!' he raged, and swung his cane high.

It was the signal.

Tonner and Quade grabbed for their sixguns, the herder surprisingly fast, the man in black blindingly so.

But Fallon was the nonpareil.

His matchless two-handed draw and clear was a thing of such effortless perfection that it was like watching man against boys. Great billows of blue-white smoke gushed from his levelled barrels and gunslinger Quade buckled in the middle like a man broken in half. He crashed down to his death without having got off a shot.

Fallon's smoking guns flicked at Tonner before erupting in a bellowing outrage of sound that seemed to fill the world.

The gunsmoke was thick and there were two men dead on the ground. The towering two-gun figure of the marshal dominated the scene. Yet a fierce-eyed rider with a shaggy mane of rusty hair and ponderous reflexes was angry enough or drunk enough to make a try at fumbling a rusty old gun out of leather. He stopped a bone-snapping bullet in the shoulder for his pains.

It was all over at that point. At least it should have been. Gunwise, Fallon didn't expect anybody to have the nerve to try and take the fight further now. Only a fool would do so – in this case a young and drunken fool. The marshal caught the blur of movement at the right-hand tip of the crescent-shaped mob facing him. He swung both barrels in that direction, but instinctively dropped his line of fire on identifying the boy.

Kyle Braddock screamed with the agony of a shattered thigh as he pitched backwards, involuntarily jerking trigger as he hit ground. The wild slug smacked the hitch rail below Fallon's position and ricocheted upwards to catch him beneath the jawline. It drilled its way upward into the brain.

5

TROUBLE TOWN

Jim Rand watched the last weeks of spring give over to summer.

Days, he tended the law office, exercised and fed the horses and frequently found himself doing the rounds with a jittery deputy who was biting his nails down to the quick despite the fact that since the night three men died the town had remained virtually trouble free.

He hoped it would last, as he flipped the jailhouse wall calendar before heading off for a bite at the Plains City Hotel – as Rhea Tillingham's guest.

The turnkey and the woman of the world seemed to hit it off surprisingly well, and he was relaxed in her company, though careful to avoid the topic of the marshal.

She had single-handedly arranged and funded the funeral – the biggest in Freetown's history – which she'd attended dry-eyed and unapproachable in unrelieved black.

Yet she would not discuss Fallon with anyone. Nor did she quit town as all had expected, just continued life as though nothing had happened.

She fascinated Jim Rand.

Lucky he was far too young to entertain any crazy notions about her, he mused at times. She was plainly too fierce, too independent and too much a dynamic woman of the world for any forty-bucks-a-month turnkey.

He walked out to the gulch after the meal and went through the ritual Fallon had taught him. He wasn't sure why why he bothered now the marshal was gone. Maybe this was just his way of staying connected with the dead man in some way – envisioning Fallon at times like this standing before him tall and serious, repeating over and over: 'Don't miss. Let your breath run out before you draw. Make sure of the first shot, it could be your last. Shoot straight!'

His routine completed he headed back for the Lucky Cuss where he'd arranged to meet Hud Morrow. His route led by the Rialto Emporium where he sighted Andrew Braddock sunning himself on the long porch, hands thrust deep in tailored trouser-pockets, a fat cigar going nicely as he chatted with friends, the very picture of prosperity.

Braddock was raking it in these days, and Jim knew it wouldn't concern him when things returned to 'normal'. Meaning of course the first time a batch of hellions elected to really kick over the traces and got to using Longhorn Street as their private shooting gallery again, with the town now without a marshal or even a full sheriff.

In the meantime Freetown roared and 'King' Braddock had it made, with no real concerns except maybe for his son.

Kyle Braddock was lucky to have a rich and influential father, money, connections and the sheer political clout that had enabled him to keep out of jail. The boy's trial had been a mockery orchestrated by the territory's top attorneys and his acquittal on an accidental-death finding in the Fallon affair had been a foregone conclusion.

The kid might be held in contempt by the town, and was now largely ostracized and forced to consort with the Texans. But he was recovering from his wound and was free – to notch up another win for Andrew Braddock and another blow to the law.

Rand didn't voice an opinion on the matter. He'd not been there when Fallon died. What he thought of it he kept to himself.

Several horses stood on three legs outside the Lucky Cuss, flicking flies away with long tails. The street drowsed in the heat as Jim mounted the gallery and went in, only to find that Morrow had left a message that he was tied up. A drunken Texan was trying to pick a fight with a couple of clerks from the Emporium.

Jim didn't hesitate.

He took the rider by the collar and forced him out through the swinging doors. The fellow was big and ugly. He swung a haymaker and Rand went inside it and clipped him to the jaw, dropping him like a sack of coal.

'You men!' he said to the startled group lounging

by a wagon at the hitch rail. 'Cart him round to the jail and I'll be along to lock him up.'

It wasn't until the men were on their way with their charge that Jim grew aware of just how many people had stopped to stare. He looked down at his skinned knuckles and shook his head. Were turnkeys supposed to carry on like this?

Then someone clapped and another man called, 'Nice work, Jimbo!' – and he walked off knowing that it felt right somehow. But he wasn't deluding himself. He knew if the Texans really went on the rampage, then neither he nor anybody else here would be able to hold them.

And he knew that day must surely come.

'Yeeeehaaahhhh!'

The blood-curdling yells batted to and fro between the falsefronts, sounding more like Kiowas on the warpath than Texans on the redeye. Not content with galloping the full length of Longhorn Street blasting away at rooftops, cupolas and the statue of the Civil War hero, the riders from the southlands herd whirled their foam-flecked mounts at the cross street and came roaring back again, guns thundering, hoofbeats thudding like war drums.

Fearful faces peered from windows and doorways as a ricochet screamed off a metal downpipe and chunked into a rocking chair on the gallery of the Prairie House Hotel where an elderly citizen had been seated just minutes before.

The hardened denizens of Diamond's adopted the optimistic view, even as glass shattered somewhere and several more Texans joined in the main street derby. It had been too quiet and unnaturally peaceful before, they reasoned; it was likely a good thing if the herders could let off a little steam and not bottle it up. Healthy.

By sunset the whole town knew this breakout was much more than that. The outfit presently loading its cattle down at the pens were hard-nosed North-haters from a remote corner of West Texas with grudges to exorcise and compatriots to avenge, and they were nowhere near through having their 'fun' at Freetown's expense.

The turnkey and the deputy were rounding up some loose horses on River Street in the half-dark when gunfire erupted from one of the clapboard honky-tonks down by the bridge.

'No, forget it, Jim,' Ketch insisted as Rand turned towards the racket, which sounded more like firecrackers than Colt .45s in the muffling night.

Jim shook his arm loose. 'We've got to at least see what's happening, man. C'mon.'

On reaching the corner they immediately sighted a large group of herders holding some kind of hoo-raw on the vacant lot between Hammerton's wood-yards and the clapboard honky-tonk they called the Sink Bucket on River Road. Blazing torches illuminated the figures of lurching men in big hats and flapping chaps both afoot and on horseback as they flipped empty bottles into the sky and then cut loose with their .45s, spurred on by applause drifting from the windowless saloon.

'See, told you, boy. Cowpoke horseplay is all.'

Jim stood with hands on hips saying nothing. His jaw was set hard and tight creases showed at the corners of his mouth. This was exactly the kind of hoo-raw the marshal had cracked down on hard before it might develop into something more serious.

Then he sighed. He was a realist. No point in expecting the deputy to walk in Fallon's footsteps. Nobody could.

'OK,' he grunted, turning to go. 'Let's go collect the horses and . . .'

At that moment the slatted doors of the dive banged open and an ashen-faced dealer came rushing out into the street pursued by a bareheaded, bearded herder clutching an axe and shouting obscenities.

The drunks in the yard howled encouragement and it was when one beanpole astride a half-wild red stallion took off across the wagon ruts to head the terrified dude off that Jim went to intervene.

'Get back!' he shouted to the horseman, and was winning the race to reach the man first, when he moved into the full glare of the torches and was identified.

'Hey!' a thick voice twanged. 'That there's a jailhouse rat. Hey, Lucky, look out or the big bad turnkey's gonna git ya, boys!'

The shout was greeted by laughter and curses, and Jim was still some twenty yards short of the stumbling gambler when the rider on the red horse cut between them, then chopped his mount back in on him like he was hazing a steer.

Jim seized the rider's leg and was attempting to

twist him out his saddle when he was struck from behind by a runty black mustang travelling fast. Sent flying he rolled three times before struggling to his feet with his head rocking to the storm of fresh gunblasts.

He found himself ringed by horsemen showing their big snaggled teeth in the torchlight as they blasted at the sky and laughed at him. Jim's head rang and there was blood in his mouth as he dodged the short charges of first this horse, then that. They were toying with him and that was hard to take. He found himself foolishly, recklessly wishing he'd brought his gun while at the same time the sober side of him was whispering; 'And what would you do if you had it, turnkey? Get yourself killed?'

'Maybe not,' he grunted aloud, then suddenly glimpsed an opening in the circle. He darted through it and was surprised to find Ketch waiting there on the fringe of the mêlée. He seized hold of Jim and began dragging him off to safety.

'Goldang, looks like the little dogie's gonna git away on us, pards!' hoo-rawed the derisive beanpole astride the blood-colored gelding. Then he jerked trigger to throw up a spray of mud over both men's legs, and he wasn't funning any longer. 'Git while we're in a good mood, Yankees, or you'll be gittin' what your butcher lawdog give the Tonners and Quade. Heeyahh!'

Jim allowed himself to be led away. His lungs were pumping like bellows and he burned with shame and anger when he found himself refusing to look to see what had happened to the dealer. What point was there? He couldn't help him. With Fallon gone, there was nobody in this town who would or could.

That day yet another burning south wind came blowing up out of Mexico to torment the Big Bend country as it did two days out of three this time of year, then drove far into the north to broadcast its gritty misery far and wide across the vast and unfenced Yellow Sky region of vast and parched Mesquite County.

The men riding the endless steppes of Amos Elder's kingdom of dust, thornbrush and maverick cattle seemed indifferent to gritty eyes and sand in their teeth, so accustomed were they to it all. Days like this doors and windows had to be shuttered tight, and the hands didn't eat until they returned to headquarters where they might at least have a chance of sitting down to something without sand in it.

There was a gray similarity about the men who worked the remote Sand Hills sector of the huge spread that oppressive day. Whether they be Texans, New Mexicans, 'breeds or Mexicans, all were lean and humorless with faces burned dark by the sun. No mustaches, no beards, no fancy shirts, hatbands or belts. Common as dirt and plain as old saddles, anonymous riders of the range.

And bitter Confederates all.

It might not have seemed like it to an outsider, but this bunch of weasel-lean buckaroos adding to the roiling dust clouds as they dragged great bundles of beef offal behind their horses across one of the ugliest landscapes in all Texas, were working the round-up.

It was their first. Up until the railroads came West

the Southerners here only caught and killed suffi-
cient beef for their needs. Now they were rounding
up night and day with a unique technique that had
come all the way from Tennessee.

The Yellow Sky was so vast and the cattle so feral
that any conventional round-up would have taken
forever – and the dour veterans of Elder Ranch who
hadn't seen cash money since Appomattox, might
well have stayed that way but for Elder's familiarity
with the 'blood muster', plus a certain bloody incident in the north.

It wasn't until fellow rancher Sam Kittleson
returned to Yellow Sky with the grim news of the
death of his two nephews and a Texan gunman at the
hands of a Yankee marshal up north, that Elder
suddenly found himself with a cause he could get his
teeth into. Revenge. But it had to be done right; it
had to be financed – hence his decision to round-up,
drive to a place called Freetown, transact his business
then exact Texas justice, his way.

The blood round-up had been in progress for
weeks now. It comprised individual parties travelling
in different directions across the limitless landscape
dragging lures which left the scent of blood, until
they sighted a bull with some cows and calves. The
smell of blood enrages a longhorn bull. At first scent
he paws the earth and acts up violently in a way that
attracts his herd, and then the whole bunch will set
off to follow the trail to its source.

One by one, bunch by bunch, the bull herds would
follow the lures across the trackless miles to the huge
box canyon in back of the headquarters, from which

there was no escape once the mesquite-disguised gates were dropped into place behind them.

That day the tally his ramrod delivered to Elder at his soddy house, set in the flank of an ugly brown hill a mile above the canyon, stood at 1,150 head. This was also the same day a rider completed the five-day return journey to the nearest one-horse town and brought back a newspaper trumpeting the six-weeks old news of the appointment of a new gun marshal at Freetown.

Elder took the news personally. Six foot two of spare-bodied shambler, he came of the same forests, hills and backwoods from which Jeff Davis, Calhoun and Jackson had sprung. He'd lost the war, lost his home, had even lost the right to live in the towns like other men because of his violence and hatreds.

When Kittleson came back with his grim news from the north, Elder had vowed to wind up his round-up quickly and drive north in quest of revenge. He had been ready to do just that when, again belatedly, they heard that although Fallon had been killed no killer had been elected to take his place up in Freetown.

He'd still planned to deal with that outpost of Yankee hatred, but there was less immediacy, so he'd continued adding to his swelling herd until today when he found himself studying a yellowing newspaper bearing a heading that read:

MARSHAL HOLLISTER TOWN'S HERO!

Illiterate as a bedpost, Elder was obliged to have

Kittleson read him out the details of how Fallon's 'protégé and natural successor' had swept Freetown clean and restored law and order with only the odd unlucky Texan killed in the process.

It was a long night that followed, a night in which decisions were made, supporters sent for, preparations for a one-hundred-mile drive with something over 2,000 head brought forward and completed.

The atmosphere surrounding Yellow Sky's sprawling headquarters at daybreak – under a sky strangely still and almost serene before the accursed mistral began to blow – was ominous.

Already the drovers were bringing the half-awake herd up from the holding canyon, the cookshack had been busy since long before daylight, the dark figures of riders were readying their horses, checking their guns and frequently glancing northwards where a gaunt pillar of ancient ugly stone marked the line of the trail that would lead them all the way to their date with destiny.

It was an unusual sight on the Yellow Sky to see lifelong henchmen Kittleson and Elder looking almost happy. It was an illusion, of course. Neither man had ever been happy. But they did feel good. They were bitter men with a cause they chose to see as almost sacred, and the time to pursue it was now.

He'd waited a long time to do what had to be done, but Freetown's replacement of one butcher with a badge with another following six weeks of permitting his fellow Texans to just as they wished up there, was the trigger he'd needed.

This day he was reflecting on the wisdom of an an

ancient saying his hard-hating mother had: *Revenge is a dish best eaten cold.*

It was bitter whiskey Jim was drinking.

'I've been to see Braddock, the mayor, Doc Sheedy from Diamond's and a dozen others tonight, Miss Tillingham,' he complained bitterly. 'Told them we need either a replacement for the marshal or to swear in maybe a dozen special deputies from the town, otherwise we'll go under. I even warned them that the next herd on the trail has an even worse name than the one we've got here for raising hell, but—'

'But you got absolutely nowhere?' the woman finished for him. There was a rustle of taffeta as Rhea Tillingham took a seat across the table from Jim Rand and her current escort, a flamboyant and amiable financier from Kansas City who was dozing in a big fat chair. The dining-room was closed, the silent staffers clearing away quietly and nervously. The whole town was on edge as roaming gangs of Texans wandered the streets at will with the occasional blast of a pistol to punctuate their parade. Jim wasn't surprised to find Rhea completely composed and relaxed as she crossed one silken leg over the other and sipped from a glass of red wine. He would be surprised were it otherwise.

'Yeah,' he continued, leaning back wearily. 'Noplace. Braddock's the stumbling block, of course. This is what he's wanted all along ... a roaring boomer with no rules. He's got his businesses well protected and bodyguards to keep him safe, so what does he care? Nobody seems to . . .' He paused, then added deliberately, 'Since the marshal, that is. He cared.'

'Oh yes, he certainly did.' Green eyes glinted as Rhea opened a small black evening purse to extract a packet of Turkish cigarettes. 'And look where it got him.'

He studied her in silence. They rarely touched on Fallon, even obliquely. But his curiosity was strong.

'You know, Miss Rhea, I guess I expected you'd be quitting Freetown after the marshal was killed.'

'Oh? Why should I do that? I came here to make money. I know many here believe I came here because Gil and I were friends. The truth is, we were both here for the same reason. This is a boom town, a place where one can make money, as I do, or be in great demand, as was Gil.' A shrug. 'I'll stay here until I get bored or go broke.'

'What makes me feel that's not the true reason you haven't left?'

'How perceptive of you. Very well, if you must have the truth, I'll give it to you. I am staying on in the faint hope that by doing so I might get to see what is it about this speck on the map that any man in his right sense would be prepared to die for. Perhaps you could shed some light on that mystery for me, Mr Rand?'

Jim poured himself a quarter-inch of whiskey and, turning it in his hand, frowned pensively at the flat tilt of the liquor.

'I grew up here, Miss Tillingham. I ran these streets as a kid. I love it.' He looked up. 'But that's not the reason it's special. It's special because it's the West. This town, another town, they all start off the same way and they've all got the right to grow strong, prosperous and peaceful. It sticks in my craw – others' too – that fine places like Freetown can be taken over by bloodsuckers like Braddock or haters and wreckers like the Texans and turned into trash. Maybe that's why some might reckon it's worth dying for.'

'Er, ahhh, well said, young Jim,' grunted the financier, coming awake and reaching for his glass. 'Don't you agree, Rhea?'

'Be quiet, Randolph,' she said. She treated her admirers shabbily, Jim noted. That was her style. So different from the way she'd been with the marshal. She smiled across at him and added, 'But yes, I suppose you are more articulate than I thought.'

There was no reading her expression now as she rose and moved back to her window.

'Well, perhaps I can understand someone with ties, as you have here, feeling as you do. But why should an outsider think it worth dying for?'

He rose and picked up his hat.

'The marshal reckoned the law was worth dying for, ma'am. I happen to agree with him.'

She turned in a swirl of taffeta, blazing-eyed.

'And is that why you continue in that stupid dangerous job – associating yourself with the law? Because you want to die? Look at you right now. All scuffed up and knocked about for the second time in a month. The Texans hate this town because of what's happened. I have heard there are obsessed cattlemen down south with plans to make an example of Freetown because of what's happened here. Dangerous, embittered men. And they'll do what they threaten. So what is Gil's legacy worth in light of that?'

'I've a hunch you know exactly how much it's worth, Miss Rhea. As for me, I'm no town-tamer, not even a lawman. I guess the only thing I shared with Marshal Fallon was knowing what was right.'

'I can offer you a job here,' she called after him as he made for the door. 'A safe job.'

Hand on the knob, he forced a grin as he looked back. 'Then we'd be without a marshal and a turnkey. Thank you kindly for the offer, Miss Rhea, but I guess I've got to stick for a while longer.'

'Then die if you want to. Go on, get out, Jim Rand. I can tell you I'm sick of the smell of dead men. And do you know why I'm so certain I will live to see you dead?' Her red mouth twisted with emotion. 'Because Gil confided to me once that you were just like him, thought like him about things ... even boasted that you were what he called a natural with a gun. He actually seemed proud while I was simply disgusted. So ... go and hurry up and die, why don't you?'

'Night, ma'am,' he replied softly, and went down the stairs feeling curiously strengthened by what had been said between them – said and understood. Went out into the street – his street. Walked proudly and confidently through the uneasy night of his town.

6

ALONG CAME A STRANGER

A long train of cattle cars rolled into the yards on a hard-blowing day of heat and dust a month later, by which time 3,000 longhorns were grazing out at Burnt River Valley and Freetown was overrun with herders end to end.

Following the stock train down from Buffalo Haunch and the East–West line came a flashy Schenectady-built 45-tonner loco, with gold-painted smokestack and shining silver wheels, hauling four passenger-coaches and a red caboose. From it poured a flood of people of the new time, dudes in hundred-buck suits, women with ostrich-plumed hats and painted faces, wheeler-dealers, dudes, gambling kings, drifters, crooks and Pinkerton men, failed entrepreneurs and black men with gold teeth and stilettos in their boot tops in case of trouble.

North met south at Diamond's, the Lucky Cuss, the Bull's Head and the Last Chance, the hard-timers quickly finding their place along the mean streets down by the yards. Those with flair and money to spare checked in at the Main Street hotels, showing a preference to dine in style and luxury at the Plains City where Rhea Tillingham offered a touch of class along with an intriguing romantic connection with the town's violent and widely publicized recent past.

Everyone had heard about the love-hate relationship between the Texans and Freetown, yet things seemed peaceful enough to the newcomers who saw that the law was little more than an office with four cells with rarely anybody in them; a paper tiger in a town where Texans and wheeler-dealers now ran the show.

This Freetown was the realization of the dreams of the entrepreneurs responsible for building the spur, yet ironically as the days rolled by on a full head of steam, fuelled by new money, it was the man most responsible for the changes who appeared curiously glum and pensive as he made his way along Longhorn for the council chambers.

'There must be some way of doing it,' Braddock said, thinking out loud as his party was forced to stop for a horseman hammering by at the gallop. The dirty, grinning, buck-toothed face of a Texan leered down and emitted a rebel yell.

'Do what?' panted Kyle. He was in poor condition.

'Get hold of their money without having to put up with them.'

Some chuckled. It was often hard to tell when he

was serious or not. As usual, Braddock was accompanied by his retinue of bodyguards and flunkeys along with his son who greeted passing Texans by name and scowled at most of the locals they met along the walks.

The big man was still brooding over an incident of several nights back at Diamond's when a brawl amongst rival gangs of cowboys almost destroyed one of his places. Several people had been wounded in that ruckus. This concerned Andrew Braddock not at all. Yet during the brawl a stray bullet had snored directly over his head while he was observing from what he'd considered a safe distance from a landing.

Scared and outraged he'd immediately summoned the saloon's full complement of doormen to deal with the offenders, resulting in a real donnybrook that had ended up costing him over a thousand in damages plus several men laid up with injuries.

The 'cowboys' paradise' that Braddock had always envisioned for Freetown was a reality but, much as he hated to concede the point, things seemed in imminent danger of getting out of hand.

The proposition he put to his fellow committee members a short time later took most by surprise. Braddock was advocating signing on several additional deputies to support Monty Ketch, who was doing little more than keeping the chair in the front office of the jailhouse warm these days.

After some debate it was decided to follow through with the proposal and everybody quit the building feeling that a prudent and sensible decision had been made and acted upon, reassuring one another they'd all get together again that same night for the opening of Freetown's biggest and plushest saloon and gambling-hall yet, the Palace on Carney Street.

In retrospect it would appear that the men who ran Freetown had come to a sensible decision, even if they might have acted sooner.

'How's it goin', Jimbo? Hey, is it true what I hear that they might be hirin' some new deputies, and you'll be offered a star?'

'Just talk, I reckon.'

'Would you take it if it was offered?'

'I'll let you know if it happens, Buck.'

Buck Wells looked at him closely. 'You seem kinda down, pard. Let's have a shot.'

'Maybe later.'

'Whatever you say. *Adios, amigo.*'

The broad-shouldered blacksmith vanished in to the Bull's Head which seemed to be heading for an all-night wingding.

He knew he'd be dull company tonight.

The long days at the jailhouse and a feeling of impotence in the face of ever-increasing trouble were wearing him thin. He kept waiting for some major change that would either strengthen the law office or do away with it altogether. He had lumps and bruises to show for the never-ending battle to prevent the Texans from taking over completely. Not even Ketch was any help. He seemed to be carrying the burden alone. Maybe he was getting to feel sorry for himself.

With early drunks stomping-tromping the walks, and weighed down by serious matters, he didn't really expect to sleep easily when he climbed the stairs to his room, certainly not to dream. Yet he did both, and a big fine dream it was too, with Freetown nominated as county capital and a brass band oom-pah-pahing down Longhorn Street with the walks crowded with proud citizens and not a long-nosed Texan in sight.

He'd been in an argument that day in which he'd aired his favorite theme, namely that Freetown could become the finest town in the region without one more cow being shipped from its yards. He'd conceded it would not be as rich as other towns but would have true law and order which he regarded as far more important. Some had supported him while others howled him down.

Suddenly he sat bolt upright knowing something was wrong. He didn't know what it might be until he glanced at the rectangle of his window, saw the orange glow in the sky and heard the fire wagon thundering by below.

By the time he reached the Palace it was a roaring inferno of leaping yellow flame and plumes of black and red smoke rising hundreds of feet into the night sky. So fierce was the heat that the firemen were unable to get anywhere near the seat of the fire. Jim and a bunch of others chimed in to help fight the blaze but it was an hour before they had it under control, another hour before the toll was known and he learned what had happened.

Texans, of course.

Nobody knew what had started the brawl, not that cowboys needed a reason. But the fight had spread into the kitchen where a vat of oil overturned onto an oven and from that moment on it was going to be a disaster. Three people dead and eleven injured, some seriously.

They were still combing the charred wreckage at daybreak when Jim attended an emergency council meeting at which a haggard Andrew Braddock made a proposal which everyone subsequently supported but which nobody had ever expected to hear coming from him.

The man who hated town-tamers proposed they advertise for just such a man to aid and sign up some additional deputies and so hope to reclaim the streets of Freetown.

The vote was unanimous and the *Herald* ran the advertisements that afternoon, advertisements which in turn appeared in every major paper in Kansas the following day.

The outcome of the advertisement was just three new deputies, one of whom was a reluctant yet strangely proud Jim Rand. He hadn't wanted to take that big step, yet simply felt he must.

Surprisingly, Ketch insisted that Rand should draw the extra ten-spot per week as chief deputy. He had his reasons.

'I'm not cut out for this responsibility, Jim. And they won't get anybody to take the marshal's job.'

'Why not?'

'Fallon, of course. He was the biggest and they killed him. It's a death watch job and everybody

86

knows it. Marshals are like a red rag to a bull with the herders. Here's hopin' they don't get a hate on for deputies.'

'They are offering big money.'

'There just ain't enough. Not for this job.'

Jim Rand just shook his head and set off on patrol. He feared Ketch was right. Who'd want the job that killed Fallon? He'd whipped this town into shape. Now it was just a little scary to walk these same streets without him as dust from the approaching herds from the south climbed higher into the sky every day.

'And just what do you think you are doing, Jim Rand?'

Bare-chested and glistening with sweat, Jim turned to see pert and pretty Jilly Foster leaning over the smithy fence. They'd gone dancing at the Institute the night before but he'd said nothing about how he'd been filling in his spare time lately.

He lowered his hammer and moved across to the fence, leaned against it with muscles bulging in arms and shoulders. He appeared much bigger stripped to the waist, and the girl was aware of it.

'Hi, Jilly.'

He was pleased enough to see her but it didn't really show. Six weeks on from the disaster of the Palace and scarce anyone in Freetown was in high spirits unless it was the town's eternal floating population of herders. People who'd been here at the beginning fifteen years earlier now walked fearfully on the streets they themselves had built, while Monty Ketch busied himself at paperwork at the jailhouse and Rand's fellow deputies concentrated on traffic watch and issuing licences. He sometimes worked off his energy and frustrations at Buck Wells's smithy.

Dark days in Freetown. But a smile like Jilly Foster's certainly helped lighten things to a degree, he had to admit.

'Going to buy me a soda, Jim?'

'Maybe another time.'

Her smile vanished.

'What's your excuse this time?' They'd had time last night and she was plainly expecting more enthusiasm from him today. 'Or can I guess? You're either lunching with your "special friend" at the Plains . . . or perhaps you're going off to shoot that fool gun of yours by the hour. Honestly, "Deputy" Jim Rand, I don't know what to make of you these days, I really don't.'

'To tell you the truth, Jilly, I promised Buck I'd shoe three horses by sundown.'

'In that case I'll let someone else treat me at the drugstore.' She pouted. 'Someone who knows how to make a fuss of a girl.'

He frowned. 'Not a Texan?'

'You think I'd be seen dead with one of them?' She tossed her curls. 'Kyle Braddock, if you must know.'

His reaction was immediate. 'I wouldn't do that if I were you, Jilly.'

'Why? Because he's good-looking with a rich daddy?'

'He's trouble. The way he hangs around with the Texans . . . and brags now about shooting the marshal. He's nobody for you, Jilly.'

88

'Well, thank you for the advice, Mr Serious, but I can take care of myself. Make sure you give my regards to Aunty Rhea, now, you hear?'

'Jilly!'

But she was gone, and he was still watching the jaunty way her hips swung beneath that yellow summer dress when the sound of an impatient hoof slamming wallboards drew him back to work.

He half-grinned as he lifted the tongs and rammed the horseshoe back into the glowing coals. She was jealous of Rhea Tillingham and didn't realize how crazy that was. Rhea was a woman and Jilly was little more than a kid. Like him. If he was looking for romance with anybody it would likely be with someone around Jilly's age. But he wasn't, so it didn't signify anyway. With the town going to hell in a handbasket all around him, romance was 'way down the list for now.

Two hours later, as the girl had predicted, he found himself out at the gulch at his eternal practice. A month ago he'd believed he was sticking to this ritual simply because the tuition Fallon had given him was something valuable which he should utilize. Now it was different. He often carried the gun concealed when on duty these days, not for law-enforcement but for self-defence. He could see the day fast approaching when he'd be called upon to use this old banger.

Shootings and knifings were a regular part of life in Freetown this midsummer. There were gunfights over crooked dice-games, flash women and politics. The cowboys fought amongst themselves and with anybody else looking for trouble. Honest citizens locked themselves in at sundown and a rival newspaper in Buffalo Haunch had coined the term 'Fatal Freetown' to titillate its readership.

And nary a response to the $500 per week ad for a replacement marshal.

These days a man could awaken to the sound of cattle being noisily loaded at the yards and go to sleep with the thunder of gunfire in his ears, not knowing until next day if the shooting had been just some likkered up cowpuncher letting off steam, or a fatal gunfight.

Later, he remembered hearing a lone horseman come in off the west trail at a fast clip, invisible behind a man-high patch of yellow weeds, and clatter on by heading into the town.

But his mind was on other things as he followed the twist of a nameless alley down off the slope, cutting directly for the railroad tracks before right-angling for the main street.

He encountered the East–and–West general agent, the yardmaster and the general mechanic as he tramped along the tracks.

'Howdy, Deputy,' said one, and the others nodded, respectful of the star. They were big important men but nobody really felt safe these days. Not even Jim Rand.

The blended sounds of chuffing, steam, driving-rods and clanking wheels were familiar now as was the drifting loco smoke from a huge pear-shaped smokestack staining the whole sweep of sky from the yards to the northern horizon.

The spur line had brought the technology of the railroad to town, which in turn brought the Texans.

The cry for a total ban on the cattle trade was growing stronger by the day but the protesters weren't on the council, occupied no positions of power. He felt today, more acutely than ever, that by the end of the season his home-town would be just another husked-out ghoster condemned to fade into oblivion when the era of the great drives ended.

He shook his head as his eyes swept across his familiar cityscape. He saw in that moment the whole sun-washed town sweltering under a merciless sun; the streets where children didn't dare play any more; the empty homes from which good citizens had packed and left; the rooms-for-rent signs above the doorways of sleazy dives; a trapped and fearful place under a coalsmoke sky.

He didn't hear someone yelling his name until a stubby shunt loco had gone snorting by, had clattered off towards the junction where a big-bellied man in a ten-gallon was waving signal flags. Then he saw Hud Morrow from the *Herald* hopping across the tracks and calling excitedly.

'Hey, been looking for you, Jim.' He propped and beckoned vigorously. 'Uptown. C'mon, you're not going to believe what's happening. Well, get a shake on, man.'

Jim wasn't in the mood for mysteries or excitement, but it seemed easier to allow himself to be hustled off along Longhorn than to argue.

'This had better be good,' he muttered as they raised the law office. He slowed when he glimpsed the crowd gathered out front by the hitch rails. 'What's going on?' Then, 'More trouble?'

'The blue-eyed opposite,' Morrow said, tugging at his sleeve and hustling him along.

Jim looked down at his sweat-stained shirt, his work-stained Levis and the old Colt handle protruding from the waistband of his pants. He realized he'd had a long tough day and looked it every inch. Well, he couldn't be fussed about how he looked. He shrugged, tilted his hatbrim against the slant of the sun and trailed Morrow round the buzzing bunch of citizens to reach the hitch rail where he saw the horse tied up.

He propped. This was no ordinary mount but an eighteen-hand monster of a Cheyenne stallion with a fierce and rolling eye and a big Texas Spanish saddle strapped to its back, all lathered and dusted by hard travel. A gleaming Winchester jutted from a fringed rifle scabbard and as they drew closer the beast showed its teeth like a dangerous dog.

'You hustled me up here to see a horse?' he asked peevishly.

'That too,' Morrow replied with a big grin. He jerked a thumb over his shoulder. 'But there's the main attraction coming out of the bar yonder.'

Across the street a long-haired stranger appeared, walking with an easy, silky grace, as long-legged and finely built as the Indian horse with the same lean hardness and suppleness of movement.

These things Rand took in at a glance, along with snug-fitting Levis flared out over high-arched boots that had probably cost fifty dollars. He saw a flat-brimmed Stetson hat banded with a rattlesnake skin-band and twin .45s in hand-tooled red-leather holsters.

But it was the stranger's face that caught the eye and held it – stirring a vague sense of recognition. The fellow's features were lean and symmetrical, with a strong jawline and bright-blue eyes that seemed to smile even though he was sober as the mob made way for him. And Jim heard the water-carter say breathily, 'So that's Hollister?'

Hollister! The nickel dropped. Photographs and sketches of the renowned law enforcer were regularly featured in the *Herald* and papers all over the region. This man had a reputation rivalling Fallon's; indeed, as Jim Rand knew well, he had put in one whole winter in Montana fighting the vigilante gangs with the late lawman two years earlier.

He was impressed, intrigued, but still didn't catch on until the flashy new arrival bounded up onto the jailhouse porch and struck a vesta off an upright, then paused before torching a cigar.

'Well, folks,' he stated amiably, 'I just told the mayor I'm in town. Now it's up to the council, I guess.'

'What the . . . ?' Jim puzzled.

Hud nudged him hard.

'Told you you wouldn't believe it, Jimbo. He's answered the ad in the papers. Chain Hollister's offering to take up where Fallon left off! Don't that beat all?'

7

MEAN WIND FROM TEXAS

'Want the brolly over you, boss?'

'Go to hell with your damned brolly. What do you think a man is? A nancy?'

'No, sir, Mr Braddock. Not you.'

'Don't crawl.'

'No, sir.'

The Texas saloon stood a full three blocks west of the Braddock house and despite the misting rain that had begun at nightfall Andrew Braddock insisted on walking to his appointment with the mayor when he might have taken his carriage.

There were reasons for this decision, for although the big man had quit his residence firm in the conviction that he would oppose the Hollister matter with full vigor, he still felt the need for more time to give his thoughts a little extra time to air, to breathe.

It was to prove a significant journey.

On Braddock's left walked a bodyguard holding a large black umbrella over his employer's head. His son was on his right with the light mist beading his dark tailored coat with fine droplets.

Four expressionless men with gun bulges beneath their jackets marched silently behind father and son. Six weeks earlier he'd only required two bodyguards. Although Braddock and his establishments were seen as aggressively pro-Texan and therefore relatively safe from that faction, such was his wealth and his reputation for dealing viciously with anyone who crossed him – Kansan or Texan – his security net seemed destined to expand in direct ratio to his bloated profits.

Braddock was raking it in with both hands and intended that things would stay that way. But despite his self-assurance he hadn't travelled half a block that night before doubts and uncertainties he'd been suppressing for a long time unexpectedly began to intrude.

First sour note was the sight of the darkened windows of the City Billiard Parlor, formerly operated by a close friend of Braddock's, now deceased. Texans.

Then there was the spectacle of the jailhouse with an uneven line of bullet holes pocking the façade following a 'ride and shoot' competition between rival cowboys in which the law building had been the prime target.

The tycoon compressed his lips and quickened his pace. His lady wife was urging him to sign Hollister on before there was a real disaster. His mistress had quit town last Saturday after a man tried to rape her – no prize for guessing where the offender hailed from. Despite these influences, he still believed a man should never pay too much heed to women, but when it came to a man's son – now that was very different.

His mood deepened when, a block further on, a buck-toothed herder with a huge buffalo gun slung across his saddle before him rode by, and bawled, 'Hi there, Kyle kid! How's the boy? You be showin' at Maisie's later?'

'You bet, Hank!' Kyle replied, and moments later swept off his hat and made a mocking bow as two of Kate Dixon's fancy women sashayed by beneath garish parasols. 'Hey there Maisie, Ella Jean, where are you two off to without inviting me, huh?'

By the time they were crossing the next street Braddock was dragging his two-tone shoes in the thin mud. His son and his habits comprised a problem he'd been trying to ignore for a long time, yet suddenly found himself compelled to face up to.

His son seemed headed for Hell on a handcart.

The more Texans who poured through town and the greater the profits he made the worse he seemed to get. Of course Kyle had alienated himself from the entire town over the Fallon affair, and as a consequence of this had been driven to seek the society of the Texans who accepted him as kind of hero – with money.

This couldn't go on. But how best to stop it? He had an uneasy feeling he already knew the answer to that. As the party gained the saloon porch, the father halted and slung an arm around the son's shoulders.

'Hey, don't start getting mushy on a man,' the boy protested, and shrugged him away to set off after two cowboys and a girl with a careless wave. 'See you later, Pa. Don't be hard to find as I'll most likely run out of *dinero* before the night's out. Hey, Texicans, wait for me.'

Braddock watched the group out of sight with a thoughtful eye then headed through the crowded barroom to the diner in back.

It was there that a clutch of assembled councillors would shortly get to bear astonished witness to his signing the official authorization for Judge Medley to swear in one DeChain Hollister as the new city marshal of Freetown.

The hotel desk clerk blinked at Jim Rand, then looked at the clock.

'Five-thirty! Seems you're rising earlier and earlier these days, Jim. Check your mail?'

Jim nodded and leaned an elbow on the desk. It was damned early, but what was the point in staying in when a man was wide awake. Why that was so he wasn't dead sure, but certainly had a notion.

You couldn't dump a Chain Hollister in any town without it shaking the hell out of it.

He half-grinned at the thought. He liked Fallon's protégé and sensed it might be mutual. Of course, how the man would go on the streets was yet to be tested.

His mail comprised a brief note from Rhea Tillingham asking him to visit.

He thought about her as he went out into the half-dark of the new morning. Although in the habit of stopping by at the Plains City Hotel for a drink and a yarn – always skirting Fallon as a topic, of course – he had not spoken to the woman since the swearing-in ceremony at the council chambers. He'd heard yesterday that she might be selling up and moving on, which was something he'd need to look into.

He wondered what she thought of Hollister's appointment.

Then he remembered.

Monty Ketch had told him he'd heard a whisper that Hollister wanted Jim Rand as his deputy marshal.

Crazy, he told himself as he strode east. For one, he was just a junior deputy with no ambition to be anything more. Two: why would a big man who barely knew him want somebody like him as his back-up in a town that had become one of the most dangerous in the West?

Maybe he was just drinking too much coffee these days, he finally decided. That was why he was up early. So, defiantly, he headed off to the early-opening Lone Star Eatery for another hot joe and a slab of pancakes.

Was it imagination or were they treating him differently at the Star? Seated at the counter, idly flirting with the proprietor's daughter, he glanced over his shoulder several times, finally nodded to himself. No doubt about it. Men were watching him; friends and acquaintances and a scatter of sullen-eyed Texans with crippling hangovers and bad attitudes. All staring.

'What's going on?' he asked the girl.

By way of reply she reached out and tugged his lapel back as though expecting to see something new pinned to his shirtfront.

'You too?' he asked sharply. 'You've heard that dumb story, haven't you?'

'Everybody's heard, Jimbo. Howcome I never knew you wanted to be a big-time lawman?'

He took his pancakes with him and finished them on his way to the jailhouse. The outsized Cheyenne horse was already tethered to the hitch rail and eyed him like he was a Kiowa horse-thief, sneaking up on him through the tall grass of the prairies with a scalping-knife clamped between his teeth. Hollister appeared in the doorway as he mounted the steps.

'Have you heard . . . ?' the man began, then flipped his flash-hat back and grinned. 'Uh huh, I can tell by your look you have. Well, cheer up, Deputy, there's worse things than being my deputy, don't you know?'

'What's the game, Marshal?'

He thought he was being ribbed. He was both angry and proud at once. But mostly he was curious. Real curious.

'How many reasons do you want? OK, I'll give you three. One, I need someone to watch my back, and Monty's not that man. Two, I like the cut of your rig. But I reckon you'll like the third reason best. Gil recommended you.'

'What?'

'You knew he and me were pals, didn't you?'

'Sure.' Jim sounded vague. Hollister's statement had rocked him. He recovered. 'But I guess I still find that a bit hard to figure on account you're both so different, you and him.'

Hollister's flashing grin showed.

'Sure we were. Gil was the serious sincere breed of lawman. I'm more your flashy, show-off type. But that man was my friend if ever I had one. We kept in touch from the time we rode Montana together right up to his murder . . .' Hollister paused, blue eyes frosting, staring off. Then, 'He said in one letter you reminded him of me when he first took me on as his sidekick.' He spread his hands. 'So, what do you say? We got a deal?'

It might have been providential, or perhaps simply coincidental, but as Jim deliberated, both dazed and flattered, he saw, above the traffic in the street, a familiar buggy go spanking across Longhorn and disappear. He knew what he needed to do.

'I'll be back, Marshal,' he said, and was gone before the other could protest.

Freetown's Boot Hill comprised a scatter of bleak tombstones dotting several acres of bleak sycamore slopes out by the river beyond the obscuring rise of One Tree Hill. He glimpsed the shiny buggy tied up at the rusted iron gates as he approached, then the unmistakable figure showing dark and slender against the large white-painted marker the citizens had erected to honor Hollister's predecessor.

She did not turn as he crunched up the gravelled drive, but spoke before he reached the graveside.

101

'Why ask me?'

He halted with a frown. 'Pardon, Miss Tillingham?'

She turned. She'd placed flowers in a glass vase. She no longer wore black.

'You know you'll take the job, so why bother asking my opinion?'

He scowled, folding his arms. 'So, you've heard too?'

She came towards him. Their eyes were on a level. She nodded.

'Yes. And I can see it in your eyes as I did in Gil's and as I do in your new hero. You all want to die. Well, go ahead. Pin on that piece of tin and buckle and go sign up. But while you're out here, why don't you select a plot for yourself?'

She strode past and he followed her back to the rig.

'I figured you'd be glad Marshal Hollister showed up. You said just days ago that it was getting too dangerous to walk down the street since we lost Marshal Fallon, but maybe Hollister and me working together can turn things round.'

Rhea Tillingham fitted one booted foot into the scrolled metal step and climbed into the buggy to seat herself gracefully, eyes on the distant town past the ugly bulk of One Tree Hill. She was silent for a time then seemed to sag a little.

'Very well, if it's important to you. Sometimes . . . sometimes I get tired of playing the cynic who's seen it all . . .' The regal, sculpted features were softer as she turned to gaze down at him. 'Do it, Jim Rand.

Take the star . . . and good luck. You'll need it.'

The slap of reins and the quick stutter of hoofs drowned out his response as she wheeled away too fast, scattering pebbles.

He was not sure why, but he knew he felt better by speaking to her before making the biggest decision of his life.

Judge Medley swore him in at the jailhouse that night and a short time later he was a deputy marshal, walking from one overcrowded saloon to another in the company of the town's new lawbringer.

The night wind blew a spatter of sand into the Texan's big teeth and he spat it right out again on a stream of yellow tobacco-juice.

Amos Elder, looking like a grim, saddle-galled, back-country evangelist, shifted a seated cowboy out of his path with the toe of his boot and moved closer to the camp-fire.

The waddy looked sullen but made no protest. Nobody seemed to be griping nearly enough and Elder wished it was different.

Yellow Sky lay fifty miles back in their dust and reality was beginning to hit home for some of his fellow ranchers and their men who'd joined the drive at the last minute.

Standing at his camp-fire that night, a hundred miles from anyplace on the sandy beach of a vast sea of resting cattle, Amos Elder could see it, smell it, feel it.

They no longer spoke as much about what lay ahead as they did of what they were leaving behind, as he'd cynically noted over recent days. A sneer flicked at the edge of his mind. Maybe this was why they'd lost the war, he reflected sourly. Too much Southern jawbone at the outset and not enough Southern pride and guts at the end when push came to shove on the battlefield.

Small wonder they'd been kicked out of Tennessee. He'd kick them off this drive if he didn't need them and their guns.

He turned his head, searching for Kittleson whom he'd sent off on an errand to the chuckwagon. These weak sisters needed a pep talk, something to lift their balls up out of the sand.

His bleak eyes cut south. Where were the three specialists he was expecting, anyhow?

The weary cattlemen rose respectfully when Kittleson showed up a short time later accompanied by two gunpacking cowboys, all three with bandannas drawn up over their noses against the dust. The rancher passed Elder the grainy framed photographs of three young dead men, which he in turned passed on to them.

'Willy Tonner, Sam's nephew and a fine boy – cut down in his prime,' he stated in a voice like rock rolling over corrugated iron. 'Next. Willy's kid brother, Kit – slaughtered like a steer at a barbecue. Another nephew and mebbe my son-in-law-to-be if he'd lived. And this one, Emil Quade. You all knew Emil. Chain lightnin' with a gun and brave as Robert E. Lee. Rottin' in the Freetown Boot Hill now. Take a good look and remember.'

One by one the somber cattlemen looked as

ordered. But Elder could tell his gee-up wasn't having the desired effect. Seemed the pictures of dead Texans was only helping them see how easy it might be for them to get dead in sunny Freetown.

Elder lost his temper. It was something he did very easily. Why didn't they just saddle up and head back to Yellow Sky? he wanted to know, ranging up and down by the fluttering fire-flames. Better to run up the yellow flag and quit out here than later on the main street of a stinking Yankee town. Cowboys began to drift closer to listen, jaws hanging loose. Once wound up Elder didn't seem to know how to stop, and some of the men began to wonder if maybe their leader mightn't be experiencing a weakness in the bowels himself as their destination drew closer, was trying to cover it by bellowing and cussing.

Finally Kittleson got him to calm down and all were seated morosely round the fire an hour later, hardly talking or meeting one another's eyes when horses sounded beyond the bulk of the chuckwagon and moments later a herder with a rifle appeared followed by three men on tired horses.

Amos Elder was fifty-five years of age, yet sprang to his feet like a stripling as the riders drew rein and the leader swung down.

'Boys!' he boomed. 'At dog-burned last. What in hell kept you?' He grabbed the dark-eyed man by the shoulder and flung a gesture at the ranchers, now coming to their feet. 'So, didn't I say they'd be here. Now git your lousy hats off and say howdy to Conn Sheran and his boys from Flint Ridge.'

The camp-fire flared and by the sudden burst of

light the Texans saw that it was indeed Sheran the outlaw, gunslinger and fugitive whom they were looking at for the first time in half a year and more. The man who'd once worked as a hand on Yellow Sky before he killed one man too many and the Rangers put a price on his head, forcing him to vanish into the brutal Flint Ridge country, was a young man with old eyes who moved with the suggestion of a coiled spring in his body. As he stood before them with a queer, crooked smile lifting the corners of his mouth, the firelight caught his Colt handles visible beneath his black coat, and winked off the silent challenge of crossed cartridge rims.

'Evenin', gents,' he said in a surprisingly deep voice, then looked at the towering Elder like he was an equal, even a tad less, maybe. 'We said we'd come and we're here. So when do we kill this stinkin' marshal?'

Amos Elder's seamed hard face worked with emotion. This was the spirit he'd been looking for!

He immediately sent a runner off to the chuckwagon to fetch some rum, and somebody else produced a guitar and a harmonica. Soon weary red beasts were shaking their sweeping yellow horns in irritation as the rousing strains of 'Texas Forever' and 'Dixie' flooded raucously out over the sleeping herd. While the main cause for all the excitement stood apart a little with thumbs hooked in gunbelt, neither drinking, grinning or singing as he watched his fellow 'patriots' with barely concealed contempt.

Conn Sheran, twenty-seven years of age with twelve kills to his credit and with far more ambition than patriotism, was a man with his own deadly agenda.

8

RAGING GUNS

It was Saturday night and Deputy Jim Rand was in good spirits on his third uneventful week in his new job as he and Hud Morrow strolled out of Sundown Alley and approached the Lone Star Eatery, where a bunch of shadowy figures stood on the poorly lighted gallery passing a bottle hand to hand.

'Listen to this bit, Jim,' the newsman urged, squinting at the square of typesheet in his hand. 'I wrote this: "It seems to the *Herald* that the so-called Hollister experiment is paying off handsomely with violent crimes way down and a general feeling of reluctant goodwill between the warring parties—" '

'Watch out, boys.' A mocking voice drifted down from the eatery porch. 'It's Deputy Blacksmith on the prowl. Watch out or you might get arrested and shod before this night's out.'

The remark drew sniggers and Jim paused to return the stares of a group of sunburnt Texans. He wasn't riled, just curious. For that voice had been familiar and it carried no Texas twang.

Then a slight figure thrust to the fore and Kyle Braddock stood on the lip of the gallery, swaying and smirking. He hefted the bottle in his hand.

'Arrested, shod . . . and mebbe even docked and checked out for colic. That is the risk these maverick boys are running if they mess with you. Isn't that right, Rand?'

Jim just nodded and moved on. Nothing to be gained by rising to any bait put down by Braddock's liquored-up son. Mocking laughter followed him.

'Got him buffaloed . . . told you I did, boys.' Kyle boasted to his companions, the only real 'friends' he had left in this man's town now. 'Now maybe you'll believe it when I say I've got this whole dirty town bluffed. And why not, Texicans? Huh? After all, you're looking at the man who beat the unbeatable Fallon, right?'

Morrow made a grab for Jim's arm as he whirled to go lunging back but was too slow. His face white, Jim shot out his arm to seize Braddock by the jacket to haul him violently down off the gallery. He spun the man roughly and slapped him hard to one side of his face, then the other.

'Your filthy mouth will land you behind bars, Braddock!' he hissed but got no further. Morrow's shout of warning from behind came too late. Something hard and metallic clipped the back of his head and the streetlights spun in his vision as he dropped to all fours, grunting as a livid Braddock closed and drove a vicious kick into his short ribs.

Dazed but conscious, Jim was berating himself for reacting after all. His fingers felt thick and clumsy as he felt for his gun, but something – most likely a cowboy boot – clipped the side of his head and poled him over onto his back.

He was dimly aware of Hud shouting and struggling to hold the cowboys back as they came off the gallery. He raised his elbows to protect his head against the expected battery which didn't come. The drunken shouting petered out abruptly and a pair of flashy striped pants crossed his blurred vision. A cheerful voice.

'Boys, boys, where are the manners? Now back up or you and me are going to come to it, and you don't want that, do you?'

It was Hollister, come from nowhere. The man was intimidating his attackers and moving them back simply by his presence, with the exception of one. A heavy-set waddy with a reputation, the bearded wrangler stood his ground, and when the smiling marshal wagged a finger in his face he slapped it aside with a curse.

Next moment the Texan was on his back clutching his jaw. Nobody had seen the short punch that knocked him down but he'd sure felt it.

In the sudden hush that followed Hollister reached down and reefed the man to his feet. A rivulet of crimson trickled from his broken mouth, his eyes were glazed over and spun in their sockets like pinballs.

Hollister, still exuding beaming goodwill to all, stepped back a pace.

'Blink for me, Texas. C'mon, c'mon, just one blink. Humor me.'

After a woozy moment, the man did as ordered. He was too dazed not to. Hollister's arms blurred and when the herder's eyes opened he found himself staring into twin sixgun muzzles just inches from his eyeballs. And a man on the gallery breathed, 'Sweet Judas! Didja see that?'

Nobody spoke. They were rough, hard-drinking illiterates of the open range who'd never met anyone quite like this.

'OK, *amigos*,' Hollister said amiably, finger-spinnng the Colts and dropping them back into the holsters. 'Show-off stuff, I know. But the point I'm getting across, is that you boys don't want to mess with any ten-cent trick shooter that can do stuff like that, now do you? So, do we understand one another?'

The Texans were mute. Framed between two big hats, the blotched face of Kyle Braddock peered out, angry and scared. Hollister shot him a cold blue stare of warning before dipping into his pants pocket to produce a ten-dollar bill.

'No hard feelings,' he said, fingering the money into the still-bleeding herder's shirt pocket. 'Go buy your pards a round or two and live it up a little, Texas. I'm sure going to.' Within moments the three Freetowners had the porch all to themselves. Chain Hollister fingered his hat back off his forehead and nodded to his deputy.

'Why make the job of shovelling out the trash hard when it can be so easy, I always say, Jimbo. C'mon, I'm on my way to break bread with Miss Rhea. Let's make a night of it.'

Although the evening had gotten off to an uncertain start, it quickly moved up the scale to good and eventually great at the Plains City Hotel. There was food, wine, music, good company and easy laughter with Rhea, Hollister, Rand and Morrow setting the pace for a twenty-strong bunch of locals, guests and visiting firemen and their ladies in an upstairs party which was later joined by a relaxed Andrew Braddock and his latest romance, living it up and apparently unaware of his son's brush with the law.

Later, Jim Rand was to view that night as an island of brightness separating the hard times behind from the trouble ahead.

Rhea Tillingham lighted a black-and-gold Turkish cigarette and moved to the window of her suite, which commanded an overview of the intersection of Longhorn and Plains. She inhaled deeply and adjusted the collar of her fashionably cut shirtwaist – just arrived from her couturier in Kansas City, special delivery. When the knock sounded she dropped her hand from the brocaded curtain and turned with a frown. The day was still young and she'd given instructions she wasn't to be disturbed.

'Yes?' she called.

'Visitor for you, Miz Tillingham,' replied the maid's voice.

'Who is it?'

A familiar male voice answered. 'It's Chain. Like a word.'

She clucked her tongue and hesitated. She was

attracted to Hollister who was so like Fallon in some vital ways yet essentially so very different. They'd had some good times together and might have more. But she liked to be the one to set up agendas and call the shots. Always.

Eventually she crossed to the door and flicked the safety catch.

'Hello,' she said casually, moving back to her position at the window. 'To what do I owe the pleasure?'

He grinned as he placed his hat on a low table. 'Hope it is a pleasure, lady.'

She studied him coolly. She'd never encountered a handsomer man but detested his profession.

'You wouldn't be in this room if it wasn't. Pour yourself a drink.'

He shook his head as he circled the big, richly appointed room. He moved like a panther, she thought, lithe and muscular. Fallon had described this man as the fastest with the Colts he'd ever seen and she found this easy enough to believe.

He joined her at the windows and glanced down. A train had just arrived to disgorge a flood of eager newcomers through the doors of the depot. A bunch of grimy trail riders guided their mounts around the statue at the intersection. There were any number of Texans in town yet very little trouble. Hollister seemed to have a way of getting what he wanted without spilling too much blood, but she supposed there was no way this could be guaranteed to last.

'I heard a whisper that you had something to tell me, Rhea?'

'You heard correctly. I had supper with a cattle

buyer last night. He told me there's a big herd a couple of weeks on the trail up from the Yellow Sky region.'

His eyebrows lifted. 'Yellow Sky? That's trouble country. Who's bossing, did you hear?'

'Elder.'

Hollister nodded slowly and moved away. 'I guess it had to come. Elder's pard Kittleson was kin of those Tonner boys, you know. The war's never been over for all that Yellow Sky mesquite country, so they say . . .'

He fell silent for a thoughtful moment, then glanced at her sharply.

'Maybe this could be as good a time as any to shut this burg down, that's if they're serious about doing it.'

He was referring to a strengthening wave of public opinion supporting a radical faction known as the Ban the Herds group which had been stridently advocating that Freetown cease catering to the Texas trade and close it down completely as a shipping center.

This faction, led by the mayor, was demanding the council seek authority through the courts to dismantle the marshalling yards and officially advertise that from herewith the cattlemen must utilize alternative railroad towns for their purposes. Several Kansan towns had successfully taken that step over the past two years. It was legal, and to many in town it made sense.

'You know full well Braddock will never allow that,' Rhea said dismissively, crossing to the opposite windows. 'And he still holds the power here despite what you and the council might like to believe.' She glanced down and pointed. 'There goes Jim. How is he making out, Chain? I mean, really?'

'He'll be fine. He's got the makings, like you said. He has a lot to learn about the game but there's iron in him, and he's a dead shot to boot.'

'I still can't believe I recommended that you sign him as your deputy.'

'I can. You care for him . . . .' He rested his hands on her shoulders from behind. 'Like I care for you, Rhea.'

'Chain . . .'

'It's OK.' He smiled, turning away for his hat. 'I'll admit I've got tickets on myself, but I'm no dreamer. I know you loved Gil and that he was the only man for you. But I'll still tell the world you are the finest-looking woman between here and the moon, and with more moxie than any man I know . . .'

His voice trailed away. The syrup didn't seem to be working. Could he be losing his touch?

'Just for once in your life, Mr Two-Bit Dude Grandstander,' Rhea said with sudden force, 'why don't you talk straight?'

'Why, I thought I was.'

'You never do, but now's the time. Let's stop the game-playing for once. Just why are you here, Chain? What prompted you to quit a thousand-dollar-a-month job at Red Medicine River to ride three hundred miles to this town and take over Gil's job for peanuts? Why? I have to know.'

He wasn't smiling now. Hands on hips and china-blue eyes suddenly flat and hard, he talked straight.

'I thought you'd figure that one, Rhea.'

'Figure what?'

'Why, the fact that he'd left his job unfinished.'

'It was only a stupid job.'

'It was never that,' he replied, drawing tobacco and papers from his pocket. 'Anyway, this was the town that killed him and I came to finish what he started so's he'd rest easy.'

He paused to lick the tobacco-filled paper into a perfect white cylinder. 'I thought you'd have understood that, lady.'

'It's not a job, it's a game,' she said fiercely. 'That was all it ever was for both of you.'

He set his smoke alight and shook out the match.

'Then why are you still here if you feel that way?'

'Money, damn you. It's a cowtown and I get rich in cowtowns, like you. Why else would I come?'

They were like two boxers, sparring, feinting, looking for the opening.

'Why?' he replied harshly. 'Because you're afraid you could've been wrong about Gil. So you came here to prove yourself right. But you missed out, honey. He was a bigger man than even you knew. Every time he walked a street or risked his life it was for the future of some place, an ideal if you like – a dream for the next decade or the next goddamn century. The law was more important to him than money, fame – even you, even if he did love you. So he died for it and I'm here to see it wasn't for nothing.'

'You're crazy. You were both crazy!' she cried, yet

with tears of uncertainty in her eyes now. Then softly, 'Did he really love me, Chain?'

'Only woman he ever could – or did, sweetheart.'

'Thanks . . . Marshal,' she said, regaining some of her composure. She straightened, dabbed once at her eyes, then was herself again as her smile gave way to a frown. 'And do try and not get yourself shot in the immediate future, will you?'

He paused in the doorway.

'You want to tell me why you're still here, Rhea? With Gil gone and all, I mean?'

'Who knows? Perhaps I'm staying to see if this place might ever become what he wanted it to be. You know – police on the corner and kids rolling their hoops down the street. That sort of day-dreaming.'

His quick smile flashed. 'It will be if I have anything to do with it.'

'Don't forget about Elder.'

'Beautiful, that kind of news isn't the kind you forget,' he said, and was gone. She heard him skipping lightly down the stairs like a kid hurrying off to some game. And thought: 'They play with death, and try to pretend it's worth it. Perhaps it is.'

To the eye of the great Sonoran buzzard a thousand feet above, it appeared as though the very earth itself was surging northward between two rows of raddled hills. But the up-close view from behind the chuck-wagon where Stone rode was that of a great tromping mass of trouble on the hoof, which was all too clearly identifiable as two thousand head of mean-tempered cows with scimitar horns and lolling tongues tramping out the endless miles in brute misery as they headed dumbly towards their bovine destiny of yards, trains, slaughterhouse.

Each slogging, slobbering beast bore a large crescent C brand on its hindquarters, and the defiantly named Crusade herd was averaging ten miles a day.

Amos Elder hawked and spat as the familiar lean figure of Kittleson emerged from the billowing red dust behind. The sweat-streaked cowman fell in alongside. Their eyes met but they didn't speak. There was no need. Each marched to the beat of the same drum. And when a rash bunch of Kiowas hit the west wing of the herd just on sundown, looking for a beast to run off, Elder and Kittleson were in the vanguard of the squad of gun-toting riders who stormed out to drive them away, as though already thirsty to spill blood.

Hollister flipped a silver dollar high.

'Heads or tails, Deputy. Winner takes the main street, the loser River Road.'

'Heads.'

The coin landed and both men leaned forward beneath the lamppost to inspect it.

'Hard luck, Jimbo, you lose.' Hollister pocketed his money and grinned. 'But just think. It's always cooler down that way around dark-down. Me? I'll be sweating inspecting all those cathouses and dance-halls.'

'Maybe I should come with you?'

'Huh? What for? Quiet night, cowboys behaving

themselves, nothing much happening down at the yards. Why would I need you to hold my hand?'

They were standing before the jailhouse where the new turnkey was just lighting the lamps. A group of citizens strolled by, nodding respectfully. Freetown had pride in its law office these days even if some might complain about the number of troublemakers, mostly Texans, who ended up at Doc Finch's when the marshal was through with them.

'Ladies.' Hollister tipped his flash hat and smiled whitely. Then, 'You still here, Deputy?'

'You're not fooling me, Marshal,' Jim said quietly, his badge winking in the yellow glow. 'You're edgy tonight. What's it about? Not that bunch from the Rio Grande, is it?'

'Hey . . . I cracked a few of their heads and that was the end to it. I'd start at East Street and work my way down to River if I was you.'

Jim shrugged and headed off along Longhorn, leaving his superior grinning after him. 'Getting too smart for his own good, that deputy . . .' Hollister murmured. Then he frowned as he flicked a speck of dust off his shirtfront before starting off, for the other had been dead on target. The Rio Granders were on his mind some, had been ever since he'd given them until midnight to get gone as a result of a brawl at the Lucky Cuss earlier.

He knew those bad-asses liked the beer and the girls at Diamond's.

It was a balmy night with a fat moon already riding the sky, and even if he was *en route* to check out a troublesome bunch, Chain Hollister wasn't taking anything too seriously as he quit Longhorn to follow a narrow back street to where the lights of the Spanish Wine Bar spilled out invitingly.

He'd promised to buy a drink for one of the dancers from Diamond's here and reckoned he had time for just one, maybe two at a pinch.

He sauntered through the batwings and everything happened at once.

A shade flew up off to his right with a sudden chopping sound like a runaway ratchet wheel.

Seated white-faced at a back table, his date screamed a warning and dived for the floor as a sixgun roared a split second after Hollister headed for the floor, the bull bellow of the old .45 sounding like God laughing in the confined space.

The marshal rolled and came up on one knee with a bucking gun in either fist. Glass shattered and the whole room seemed to explode with the big, hard, head-splitting roar as the lean-bodied Texan rifleman who'd bobbed up from behind the bar stopped three in the guts. He went rigid. The rifle dropped as he clutched at himself, red blood bubbling through his fingers. Falling backwards he disappeared with a crash as two quick shots sounded from a corridor in back of the piano.

All Hollister needed was the flare of the shots and he was triggering back with a continual storming fusillade while rolling across the bare boards at bewildering speed. The unseen ambusher gave a strange strangled cry as he ran into a brace of slugs and came reeling out into the full glare of the lights with two sudden eyes in his head and his coat tails flapping in the hard percussion of sound.

Instinct told Hollister it was over, yet he waited where he was, motionless, twin guns extended before him at arm's length and every nerve stretched taut for a full half-minute until the girl found her voice.

'There was only two, Chain. They . . . they followed me . . . knew you were coming and . . .'

'That's OK, baby,' he said, coming erect to help her off the floor. He looked around with an expression of distaste. There was so much smoke choking the dump you'd think the place was afire. 'C'mon, they can clean up here, I'll walk you back. Then there's a geezer I've got to go see.'

Twenty minutes later, and looking as calm as a man who'd just emerged from a long soaking bath, Hollister stood with boots apart upon the rich russet carpet of Andrew Braddock's private mahogany-and-leather office at the Council and Civic chambers on Longhorn Street. A cigarette jutted from his teeth and his deputy stood behind him, laying down the law according to Hollister.

'It's time,' he was repeating. 'I've had the lid on this place for two weeks, this bunch was just passing through, no need to fear they might do something loco. But they did and they'll go on doing it, unless . . .'

'Unless what?' Braddock sat behind his big desk massaging his mid-section with soft fingers. He was gaining weight. It was his biggest concern at that moment.

'You know 'unless' what. Unless you cast your vote to close down the yards and ban them. It's the only way. I saw it work at Westville, Black Crow and . . .'

The big man heaved himself erect, tugging down the points of his tailored vest.

'Marshal, if you feel you have the right to take up my valuable time and parrot the speeches I hear at every Council meeting, you have another think coming. I suggest you bury the dead and get on with what you're being paid for. Now, gentlemen, if there's nothing else . . . ?'

He was ushering them out. They went, but Hollister propped in the hallway.

'Look, Braddock, if you want to play it tough, I can do likewise. About that kid of yours. If you're not worried about what might happen in this town you should worry about him. I chip him and send him home at least twice a week funning it up with trouble riders like that pair that jumped me tonight. He takes dope and runs with whores, and Texans are about the only friends he's got left. Clear the herders out now and you might have a chance of keeping that young fool from doing himself in, but—'

'Thank you for the advice, Marshal,' the big man said coldly, striding off. 'But I do advise you stick to what you do best, namely killing people. I'll be first to acknowledge you're very good at that.'

'See what I mean about this line of work, Jim?' Hollister growled. 'It's the dregs. Want to hand me that badge while there's still time for you? Me? I'm too old or too dumb to quit.'

'Let's go settle the street down, Marshal. Then I'll go round to the undertaker's.'

Hollister gave him a long steady look. 'You know,

Deputy, sometimes I get the weird feeling you're better suited to this lousy line of work than I am myself, damned if I don't.'

We'll talk later,' Jim replied. 'They're pretty jittery down there.'

Hollister lifted his hands and let them drop with a grin. 'Whatever you say, Mr Marshal sir. Let's hustle.'

9

WHEN HEROES FALL

Hud Morrow was having trouble keeping up with events in town the following afternoon, and his father was riding him hard. He'd just completed a 2,000 word report on the gunfight at the Wine Bar for Thursday's edition and yet another covering the sudden withdrawal of the dead Texans' outfit, along with interviews and a lengthy article on the Ban the Herds movement.

Now he was expected to interview both Marshal Hollister and Jim Rand on behalf of the editor of the Buffalo Haunch *Star* up north – and couldn't even find them.

This was because at that very moment Freetown's lawmen were sprawled out on the riverbank with their fishing-rods down below the bridge where the slum quarter reached clear down to the sand bar.

They sat about ten feet apart and didn't talk, just fiddled lazily with their lines and waited for the big one to strike. Most of Freetown felt that Hollister was taking the double killing pretty casually, but Jim knew better. Truth was, he'd come to know this man almost as well as he had Gil Fallon, had learned to respect him equally.

He saw neither man as the badge-toting killers such as they were painted by the saloon sages and newspaper editors, but rather as dedicated idealists who just happened to follow a violent profession.

A wagon rumbled across the bridge and a fine shower of dust sifted down. The sun was making them drowsy, yet every so often Jim would glance the other's way and catch his eye and both would half-nod as though in acknowledgement of something unstated yet accepted.

For today they shared an instinctive awareness that this period of drowsy quiet in the wake of last night's slaughter was just the lull before the storm. But they were determined to stretch it out to the very limit, and might have succeeded had not Morrow found them. So they quit the river with the newsman without any fish and by the time they got back to the jailhouse there were over a dozen wires from various press sources clamoring for detailed accounts of the double killing.

Hollister dumped all the slips into the wastebasket, crossed his flashy boots on the desk and began giving an increasingly frustrated young reporter a detailed account of his love life.

Jim leaned in the archway of the cell annex chuckling to himself. It felt good. Standing in the undertaker's parlor late last night after seeing what bullets had done to two men, he'd doubted he'd ever get to laugh again.

Conn Sheran pushed his gray across the unnamed creek as dawn broke two days later with the first rays of the sunrise softening his features some so that he appeared almost boyish rather than brutal. But it was only a brief impression. By the time he'd climbed the bank and pointed the cayuse's ugly Roman nose due north again he looked exactly like what he had long since become. Pure killer.

He crested the rim and glanced back. Some fifteen miles away in the narrow ravine where they'd made camp after quitting the herd, Blade and Pooley would likely be just stirring in their sougans to find him gone. Fifty miles further south still, the herd would already be on the move with Amos Elder and Kittleson probably still cursing the fact that their gun-squad trio had ditched them right after the drive met up with the southbound Rio Grande crew – less the two men they'd left behind them in their graves at Freetown.

The gunfighter's gaunt face showed the flicker of a sneer as he banged his heels against the gray's ribcage to move it into a lope.

He'd detected a hint of apprehension even in Elder's old hate-ravaged face at the news of just how ruthlessly a pair of murder-minded Texans had been done to death by the Yankee marshal. But eventually both the boss man and his crew had recovered from the shock, and by the time Sheran and his pards had stolen away at nightfall Elder had them all primed up once more, using the Freetown deaths to whip them into a fresh frenzy of hatred for the old enemy.

But the gunman had seen what he'd seen, and held them all in contempt because of it. But it would have no effect on his plans. From the moment the drive was mooted, Conn Sheran had had his own private schedule planned down to the last detail, and it was so exclusive it didn't even include Blade and Pooley.

For he didn't give one solitary rat's ass for Texas honor or all the rest of the high-falutin' Sons of the South jawbone Elder and Kittleson went on with until a man wanted to puke from listening to it.

He believed only in himself and his guns, what they had achieved together and what was yet to be done.

Hollister would be number thirteen. He'd put twelve fast guns in their graves in his time and Hollister would be Lucky Thirteen.

He shook his head as he traversed a sweep of open plain under an already hot sun. He still couldn't quite believe in the renown that men like Fallon, Hollister, Masterton and the others had acquired in recent years while he'd been chasing around Mexico robbing tin-can banks and being chased by vast armies of hairy-faced *Rurales*.

He'd long craved to be part of the gun kings' glittering world of fame, big money and sixgun glory, yearned desperately to have the name 'Conn Sheran' lauded and even revered throughout the West as so many lesser talents already were.

Yet upon returning to the States, such was his

notoriety that he'd been forced to hole up in a plank hut one hundred miles from the nearest town in the remotest regions of the Yellow Sky country as hard-eyed Rangers with wanted dodgers in their pockets hunted for him far and wide.

He straightened in the saddle.

All that was behind him now. He'd escaped the lawmen's net with the drive, would soon stake his claim to his rightful status with the Colts in Freetown, then travel on north, there to reap the full rewards of the long overdue fame which was his birthright.

He believed he could achieve all of this with just one huge kill. And if the dead could only speak he could summon up twelve men who would surely have to agree.

So he rode through the day and continued on steadily as night drew a dark cloak about him. When a crescent moon tilted its horn over the borderlands he welcomed its soft yellow glow and felt the excitement begin to rise on realizing he was in Kansas Territory. He kept raising his right hand before his eyes, marvelling at the way his curling fingers reminded him of the talons of a hawk.

From the private room in back of the Texas Saloon, Hollister could hear the rise and fall in the murmur of the crowd in the bar. The town had been quiet since the shootings and he knew they were discussing everyday matters such as prices, cattle, hard times and high prices – most anything, he suspected but the things they didn't really understand, such as how greatly their town had changed, howcome their Boot

Hill seemed to be growing out of proportion to the population, why they kept renting out rooms to reporters and writers intent on making their town even more notorious.

He stared at the glass in his hand.

Must be strange whiskey he was drinking.

Most any other time he would be out there in the barroom in the thick of things, talking his head off, sparking the percenters and having a fine old time of it.

Why not tonight?

A gentle tap sounded on the door. He transferred his glass to his left hand and rested his right on gunbutt. 'Come!' he called, and one of the serving girls came in to see if he wanted anything to eat. He winked, sighed, shook his head and she left, giving her cute little bottom a flick as she went out – maybe just to remind him that he must be a bit on the dumb side to be moping in here all alone with his whiskey when just about everything a high-stepper like himself could ever want was there to be had just thirty feet away.

He half-grinned, shrugged in perplexity and was lifting his glass to his lips when he felt it.

The hair on the back of his neck lifted.

The barroom sounds had dropped away to a whisper and the noise of somebody shifting a chair sounded unnaturally loud. His blue gaze cut to the door and it was as if he felt a cold breath of air seeping in when he knew damn well the one commodity in short supply in that sweaty overcrowded barroom had to be cold air.

Then came the click of understanding.

Trouble.

He didn't question his instincts; they were too well-honed to doubt. Simply loosening his sixguns in their holsters, he rose and went out, moving leisurely through the big smoke-filled cavern of a room with his customery supple walk, the sudden focus of all eyes. The faces told him that everyone in the room – from the hawk-eyed case-keeper seated above it all with a cocked carbine across his knees down to Harry the Bum sucking beer suds from his moustache – was also aware of the abrupt change in the atmosphere yet didn't know the cause.

With the yellow-painted batwings swinging slowly to stillness behind him, he crossed the porch to find the street outside the saloon seemingly swept clean of strollers, riders, porch loafers and stumbling drunks beneath the stars.

Then he saw why.

The man stood half-in and half-out of the gallery shadow of the Lone Star Eatery. Hollister saw instantly that he was young and well-balanced and sported twin tied-down sixguns.

He nodded in recognition of an old and familiar game, and his heart began to trot.

Barely aware of the rustlings and whisperings in back of him as they crowded to the doors and windows, he stepped down into the dust and strolled to the center of the street.

The man emerged from the shadows without hesitation, deadly-looking as a prowling cougar. Hollister gave the faintest nod in recognition, not of who the fellow was, but what.

The real thing.

You could always tell.

'My name's Sheran. Conn Sheran.'

'So?'

'You've heard of me, Hollister?'

'Can't say I have.'

'Know why I'm here?'

'Sure.'

A flicker of uncertainty crossed the cruel young face. 'That's all you got to say?'

'I'll say so long. How does that sound?'

Emotions chased one another across the Texan's face. He was unsure, he was angry, then coldly committed to a deadly purpose.

'Then so long to you – you Texan-killin' son of bitch!' he shouted, and his hands flashed down. The .45s leapt like live things but were still on their sweeping way upwards as Hollister's twin cutters reached firing level and belched yellow flame.

Instantly Sheran was flung back with white-hot death impaling him. He squeezed one trigger unaimed but never heard the sound of the shot. He stumbled and fell sideways into the dust. It received him gently. He tried to speak but choked on blood.

The outlaws watched the town for two full days from the piney woods on the western slopes where they took turns at using the field glasses or rolling cigarettes.

It was from this seclusion that they watched the black-plumed horse and hearse bear their partner out along the dusty track to climb the steep single-tree hill then dip down to the cemetery where Sheran was laid to rest with only a handful of slump-shouldered Texas trailhands to see him off.

Afternoon that same day they saw the flashy yellow-wheeled buggy go clipping by, driven by somebody who, at a distance, might have been the handsomest female they'd ever seen, even if she was a Yankee.

That night in a River Road dive, Mick Pooley treated drinks and asked many innocent-seeming questions about Rhea Tillingham, Chain Hollister and Boot Hill.

By the time he quit the honky-tonk to meet up with his partner by the bridge, he knew just what they would do and how they would go about it. They might not be quite in Sheran's league with the Colts but when it came to killing both were real pros. And whereas their late henchman had lacked even a flicker of patriotism, Blade and Pooley burned with it as fiercely as even a Kittleson or an Amos Elder.

The chow might be none too flash at the Sink Bucket on River Road but it was usually quiet mornings, and a man wasn't likely to run into any of his friends down there this far from Longhorn Street.

Jim Rand ate a late steak lunch costing two bits, washed it down with two mugs of coffee, lit up a Durham and left.

With a loco firing up down at the yards and a steady flow of traffic through the streets it looked and felt almost like an ordinary day in Freetown. Normal. But he was not deceived. There were no normal days here anymore. There were just days when the undertaker was forced to put on extra help, plenty days when you could count on one or maybe two families loading up the buckboard and moving out.

Three men shot to death in three days.

At this rate, he brooded, by the time they got to close down the stockyards – that's if they ever did – there would be nobody left to enjoy the peace and quiet everyone craved so desperately.

Jim shook his head and gave himself a brief lecture. It was a rough period, nothing more. They would pull through just fine. In the meantime there were enough gripers and doomsayers about without his adding to their numbers.

He appeared almost cheerful by the time he reached the office where he found the marshal loafing in a cane-bottom chair with crossed boots up on the porch railing, his big horse hipshot and drowsing in the tree shade.

'What's doing, Jimbo?'

'Nothing much, Marshal.'

Hollister eased his hatbrim lower to shade his eyes. 'Nothing much sounds pretty good, huh?'

'Just fine,' Jim replied, lowering himself to the top step. 'Any fresh word on the Yellow Sky mob?'

Hollister was lazily shaking his head when there came the clatter of racing hoofs from further along the street. Both rose as people began shouting and screaming, and as the traffic gave way a wild-eyed horse hitched to an empty buggy came careening by, hurling up huge billows of dust in the wake of the bouncing wheels.

The lawmen swivelled their heads to stare at one another as the driverless equipage flashed by.

'Rhea's rig!' the marshal hollered, vaulting the railing in a tremendous leap that landed him in his saddle.

'Wait for me!' Jim hollered, but Hollister was already untied and storming away. Running into the middle of the street Jim watched him cut the big red into East Street and disappear, but knew he would be galloping south for the cemetery, just as he would have done; Rhea Tillingham drove out alone to Fallon's grave every afternoon around this time.

He raced for the horse yard in back. But there was no way he would catch Hollister, who was already raking horsehide with spur to go careening past the last row of houses, then out into open country with One Tree Hill soon looming ahead and Boot Hill out of his sight just a short distance beyond.

It took a great deal to throw Chain Hollister but he was riding like a man possessed as he urged the reaching animal on with voice and steel, fighting off a sense of dread, paying no attention to the blurring landscape on either side.

If anyone had hurt Rhea . . . he thought murderously as pounding hoofs carried him up the steep slope. But surely not even Texans would sink that low.

The crest loomed. A hundred yards to the right of the solitary tree stood a jumble of big gray boulders. Sunlight winked on something metallic in the rock shadows as the reaching rider topped out the crest, but he didn't see it. Didn't see the flash of the

Winchester .32 nor hear its brutal voice. Chain Hollister barely felt the bullet that killed him.

Seemed half the town followed the hearse out to Boot Hill next afternoon. The mayor delivered the eulogy and there were more wreaths than anyone could remember seeing before, many donated by the young women of the town, some of whom wept their way through the whole sad service.

And afterwards at the wakes held at the Texas Saloon and the Lucky Cuss, at the Prairie House and Plains City hotels, even at the Lone Star Eatery and down at the come-as-you-are Sink Bucket where some tender-hearted hustler had pinned up pictures of both Gil Fallon and Chain Hollister – even though fear stalked the streets in the wake of the last killing – ordinary everyday folks got up to say how they were just realizing what the town-tamers had done for them and how worse things might have been if they had never come.

Sure, there were some sneers and jeers from the ranks of the suddenly cocky Texans. But to a town in shock they made little impact. Freetown might not know what tomorrow would be like without a Fallon or a Hollister at the jailhouse, but today they were going to pay their respects regardless . . . and leathery depot hands wore black armbands as they worked and nobody pinched the serving girls at the saloons – out of respect for the day that it was.

Jim Rand didn't attend any of the wakes. Instead he patrolled the streets wearing his badge, bent on trying to create an impression of normalcy even if everybody might suspect Freetown might never see a normal day again.

Many of his wide circle of friends sought him out but he didn't really respond. Just continued walking and thinking maybe harder than he'd ever done in his life, until he reached his decision at around seven that night.

A short time later found him walking up the paved pathway to Judge Medley's front door.

'I say, Rhea, old girl, this is a bit much, isn't it? I mean, calling on a young chap at his hotel at midnight and expecting me to just sit down here twiddling my thumbs. Hardly cricket, what?'

Eustace Bruce, her current escort around town, was a traveller in fine china. Rhea was considering replacing all her hotel crockery services. Eustace stood to make a killing if she went ahead with her order and knew he should probably button up and suffer in silence. But damnitall, a chap had his pride.

'Oh, I'm so inconsiderate, Ewie.' She smiled unconvincingly as she headed for the stairs. 'Of course you can come up with me. You may carry my valise.' Then her eyes and voice snapped. 'Then come back down here and wait just as long as I say!'

The Bruce rebellion ended then and there, and Rhea was alone as she stood at door 22 clutching her satchel. Light seeped beneath the door. She knocked and a voice answered: 'Not locked,' and she entered.

Jim rose from the little table where the lamp burned. The woman merely glanced at him before switching her attention to the metal object leaning against the lamp-base.

'So, what I heard was true,' she said quietly. She placed the satchel on the bureau, then picked up the marshal's badge, studied it, looked at him levelly. 'Marshal Rand. How does it sound?'

'All right, I guess.'

'You couldn't wait for them to get the idea themselves, you had to go volunteer.'

'Look, Rhea, it's been a long day and I'm just not in the mood for—'

'I understand,' she said, raising her hands. 'I really do. And you might as well know I'm not really surprised by this idiotic thing you've done – which amazes me. I'm either getting older or I've reached the stage where I just love standing around in my pretty lace dresses waiting for the men in my life to get shot into doll rags . . . who knows?'

So saying she picked up the valise and placed it on the table before him. Her face was still bruised from the roughing up she'd taken at the hands of Blade and Pooley when they jumped her at the burial ground before flogging her buggy horse back to town to lure Hollister to his doom. But of course she still looked like the Queen of Sheba to this former blacksmith's-striker-cum-lawman.

'I only hope these bring you luck, Jim Rand,' she said in an uneven voice. 'If anyone deserves it, you do.'

Their eyes met and locked and the too-quiet night held them together for a pensive moment before she turned away and was gone, closing the door softly behind her.

He moved like an old man as he unbuckled the valise. He couldn't remember when he'd slept, or even if he'd done so. There was a feeling in his bones that he would be weary forever, yet the moment he snapped the bag open and the light fell on its contents every trace of exhaustion magically vanished.

Gil Fallon's guns!

10

I AM THE LAW

The two were the toast of Texas Town.

That was the name the herders had given to the sprawling slum-quarter on River Road below the Line where cowboys out of cash and losers looking for love in all the wrong places could get together and pretend they were back home in the Lone Star where everybody was just like themselves.

It had been a lean time for Texans in Freetown since a dumb town kid killed Fallon, and Hollister took his place. But this surely was their time to howl down at the good old Sink Bucket where the money of new heroes Blade and Pooley was simply no good tonight.

'Another round for my great buddies and pals!' slurred the rich man's son, throwing a ten-spot on the wet bar-top. He lurched and winked broadly at the barrel-bellied bartender. 'And another little poke of you-know-what for yours truly, Jason, you old clapper. Move, man, move! or I might have to sick Mick and Arnie here onto you. Eh, boys?'

Pooley and Blade just grinned toughly. The herders assured them Kyle Braddock was a friend and a soft touch and that was good enough for them. So they grabbed their free whiskeys off the bar, a waddy with a handlebar mustache proposed yet another toast to the vanquishers of that 'Texan-killing Hollister', and a happy young Braddock lurched off for the back room clutching his opium pipe ready to take another ride to fairyland.

There were but two windows in the dive and both were misted over in the early morning hours. You couldn't see out but Jim Rand could see in, and even without Rhea's detailed description of the pair who'd jumped her out at Boot Hill – one tall and dark with a scarred cheek and the other short and blocky with streaky white hair and yellow eyes – he knew he could not have mistaken Chain's killers as they accepted the plaudits and free drinks like true heroes of the blood.

Rage swirled through his head like smoke.

He remained there far longer than he'd intended, simply to rein in his emotions. He eventually did so, but only with Fallon's help; *Calm, never angry. Anger puts an extra ace in your enemy's poker-hand. Shoot straight. Don't miss. Your first shot may be the only one you'll get. Never miss!*

Drunken faces sharply turned his way as he kicked in the door and stood there with the night a black frame around him. There was no time for words. They saw a man with a marshal's star pinned to his chest and that was all two killers with blood on their hands needed to see.

'Take him!' roared Mick Pooley and lethal hands were slashing down and coming up with bucking guns in the blink of an eye as panic-stricken drinkers hit the floor and Jim Rand instantly felt a murderous stab of pain in his left arm.

He was hit but still standing. More important, he was calmer than ever before in his lifetime. He squeezed trigger deliberately and Arnold Blade, the faster of the pair, who'd just failed to kill him with two lightning shots, felt his whole chest explode as a single slug blew a chunk of his heart through his backbone. He fell back heavily against a cursing Pooley, ruining his aim.

The marshal shot the man between the eyes and it was over.

Almost.

Only somebody out of his skull on dope would have had the blind nerve to come staggering back into a room frozen in terror under sifting veils of gunsmoke, and throw himself furiously at a man with two smoking revolvers in his hands.

'Damn you, Rand, you dirty low . . . blacksmith!' Kyle Braddock raged, clenched fists flailing impotently. 'You've killed my good pards . . . these men are all my good pards . . . and you are just a dirty lousy upstart son of a . . .'

He broke off in mid-sentence, eyes rolling as he remembered something important. His hand fumbled inside his expensive jacket and he almost dropped the Saturday Night Special two-shot that winked wickedly in the light.

'Dirty . . .' he began, then Rand's right hand Colt

smashed him to the floor.

'You!' he said with quiet authority, indicating the local tally clerk. 'Go fetch the deputies and the turnkey, and tell them to bring manacles. Pronto! The rest of you stay right where you are. I'll kill the first man who stirs.'

Nobody moved. They were staring at him as though he'd just grown another six inches. Jim returned their looks through a haze of pain and unreality. It seemed unreal that he'd survived the past sixty seconds. But one thing was very real. He knew he would kill any Texan who so much as lifted a finger. They seemed to know it too.

Braddock eventually located Jim Rand at Doc Finch's where he was having his wound attended to. The ubiquitous bodyguards were forced to cleave a path for him through the crowd which had assembled there over the past hour, packing the small surgery wall to wall.

The marshal's friends were here in force.

Hud Morrow and rugged Buck Wells had shown up first, followed shortly by Red, Hogue and Clarry from the emporium where he'd played billiards every Wednesday night for years. Then there were several girls from Diamond's in their spangled dresses, Judy from the Lucky Cuss and two fishing pals from Cross Watch Ranch. Also crammed in somehow now was Burke Walker the dentist and some six or seven younger members of the Ban the Herds committee.

The place was packed solid and Jim was deeply

touched. Hurting, sure, but impressed. But none of what met his eyes impressed Andrew Braddock who was purple-faced and breathing hard as he halted behind the patiently working medico, eyes bugging from his head.

'You damned upstart, Rand!' he stormed. 'Get back to the jailhouse and release my son immediately. I mean pronto!'

'How does it look, Doc?' Jim asked evenly.

'Missed the bone, Marshal Jim—'

'Shut up!' Braddock shouted. 'You've locked up my son on some trumped-up charge that—'

'He's been formally charged with the attempted murder of a peace officer in the execution of his duty, Mr Braddock,' Jim stated flatly. 'See you in court.'

It was a full ten minutes before Braddock's flunkeys could persuade him to leave. The man seemed on the verge of apoplexy as they half-carried him out. The calmest person in the room appeared to be Jim Rand. He was in control both of himself and his town. Had to be. There was nobody else.

Someone had just told him the Yellow Sky herd was only two days drive away downtrail.

'Rand! Where is that stinking sham? Get in here right now, you mongrel before I . . .'

'Shut up in there!' came a rough voice from the office.

Kyle Braddock whimpered in his cell. He was a pathetic figure, shaking, suffering severe opium withdrawal, terrified and bewildered. How could this be happening to him? He couldn't even recall what had occurred at the Sink Bucket now. Surely they couldn't hang a man for something he didn't even remember? He rattled the bars impotently. Where was that stinking Rand anyway? And who in God's sweet name had made him a marshal?

He only began to calm some on recalling something his father had told him while visiting last night. The Yellow Sky herd was near. Sheran, Blade and Pooley had all been with Elder's herd – now all three were dead. Elder and his Texans would be after blood, so his father had confidently predicted. Rand's blood. He was totally convinced the Yellow Sky crew would chew up the marshal and spit him out, Freetown would be thrown wide open once more and he would be set free to go dance on that upstart's grave!

He smiled wonderingly, nodding to himself. What did he have to worry about?

As darkness fell that night the men from the south saw for the first time the glow on the northern horizon that was the nightlight of Freetown. Trail's end. Kansas!

The fierce old man leaning against the tongue of the chuckwagon, working heavy jaws on a cud of sour tobacco finally dragged his eyes away from that sight to study his men with a frown.

Why weren't they beating their chests and cleaning their weapons?

Three brave brothers newly dead at the hands of the jayhawker butchers. Didn't that ignite their rage? Where was their fire in the belly, their patriotism?

But slowly anger faded and reason returned. The men were simply reacting to the loss of their top guns, he rationalized. That didn't mean they lacked the guts to seek revenge. Not his brave boys. What they needed now was not his anger and condemnation but his words.

That talent of Amos Elder had never failed him, nor did it tonight.

By the time he wound up his last harangue thirty minutes later, the men of Yellow Sky were on their feet, ready and eager again as he led them in a rousing chorus of 'Dixie' in the night.

They met by prearrangement in Rhea's private rooms, the rich man and the marshal. Both men had changed remarkably over the past twenty-four hours. While Rand appeared to have expanded noticeably to fill the role circumstances had forced upon him, by contrast Andrew Braddock appeared visibly shrunken. The tycoon had called in all his markers and pulled every string in his powerful repertoire of influence in the hope of assisting his son, yet Kyle remained securely under lock and key with his trial scheduled for the following week.

The case for the prosecution bristled with witnesses, so he'd been advised by his attorney.

There were around a dozen citizens prepared to get up and swear that recent lethal events at the Sink Bucket had taken place exactly as Marshal Rand had already sworn in his deposition lodged at the courthouse.

Now even Braddock's friends were hinting that

things were looking bad for his son. Never mind what might or might not happen when Yellow Sky reached town – so his counsel had warned him – his son and heir really could swing.

Jim had arrived early at the hotel and was there with Rhea when the big man arrived. Naturally Braddock arrived in a fury, so Jim calmly rolled and lit a smoke and allowed the man to rage himself out before he took a deep draw on his quirley and delivered his thunderbolt.

There might just be a way out of this mess for young Kyle, he informed Braddock. It might not be strictly by the book, he conceded. But still . . . .

Braddock was dumbstruck for a long moment. He couldn't believe what he was hearing. The balloon of his temper burst, he shook like an aspen in a high wind.

'Are you serious, Rand?' There were sudden tears in the man's eyes. He genuinely did love his worthless son. 'Sure – sure you are. But how . . . ?' Braddock was almost begging. He was a man slowly coming apart. He didn't sleep any longer. Kyle's plight had exposed his weak underbelly. 'Please – don't play with a father's feelings, man.'

'I'm new to this job and I'm not a spiteful man,' Jim stated. He moved to a side table and picked up an official-looking scroll ornamented with signatures. 'This is the Council authority to permanently shut down the shipping arm of your railroad, which only needs your signature to make it unanimous and effective under the law. Miss Tillingham has a pen.

Sign this and the charges against your son won't be presented to the bench.'

'Th . . . this is blackmail!'

'Your boy can hang.'

Rand's face was blank as he stared the man down. He had no intention of pressing ahead with the case against Kyle should Braddock call his bluff. The boy couldn't have hurt a fly at the Bucket. Rand was bluffing, but he did it well. It was ten minutes before a whipped Braddock finally signed, as they knew he must. Within an hour an official proclamation identifying Freetown as a closed town to the cattle drives would be printed at the *Herald* and posters broadcast for public display in accordance with the statutes.

Braddock quit the suite looking like somebody unsure whether he'd been fleeced or handed heaven on a stick. Jim drank a toast in white wine with Rhea then also left before she could start in on what he should or should not do.

The herd was due mid-morning.

The sound of a poster being ripped off a pole sounded unnaturally loud in the silence. The lanky herder touched a corner of the paper to his cigarette and watched it flare in the sunlight. He held it aloft and the cowhands began to cheer, thirty bearded, unwashed men with sagging gunbelts and red-rimmed eyes, mostly afoot today and exhausted from the brutal drive yet eager to take what they'd come for.

Every window and doorway in the vicinity of the Longhorn–Plains Streets junction hard by the railroad depot and directly before the Plains City Hotel, was crammed with faces, had been ever since a tall and forbidding Amos Elder led his trail crew down the main stem with his big ugly mount tossing its shaggy head like a war horse scenting battle.

Yet despite the ominous atmosphere there was a surprising number of resolute-looking citizens scattered along the walks and standing in the mouths of the arcades, and someone had hung the Stars and Stripes from the upper balcony of the Texas Saloon where gamblers and painted women looked down defiantly upon the intruders.

The junction was crowded, blocking off traffic. But no sign of the law.

'So, where is he?' Kittleson growled from the corner of his mouth, flipping his trailhound a cracker.

'Likely cut and run,' was Elder's reply. He hipped around in his saddle, leather creaking in the tense quiet. 'Jensen, go toss a rock at that tin-can jailhouse and see if you can't scare up some . . .'

He broke off. The herder was staring directly past him. Elder whirled to see a broad-shouldered young man with one arm held in a calico sling to which was pinned a marshal's badge, emerging from a side street. The cattleman snorted disbelievingly. He'd heard Rand was young, but this *hombre* looked no more than mid-twenties, clean-cut and boyish. This was what passed for a marshal up here?

Sounds reached Jim in errant waves as he approached the danger zone. Nervous? He knew a man would have to be six kinds of a fool not to be.

Yet instead he was easy. He seemed encased in an armour of calm. It was as though Fallon walked on one side of him and Hollister on the other.

Only thing, it wasn't Gil Fallon wearing these guns today, nor was it ice-cool Chain Hollister facing down maybe the worst trouble Freetown had ever seen.

Just an ordunary man who'd been a blacksmith's striker less than a year ago.

Yet he felt anything but alone.

He halted and the silence deepened.

Then, 'You men saw those posters?' he demanded.

Elder shifted his cud from one side of his jaw to the other.

'Yo!' he replied. 'We read 'em just like we read them death notices on our fine boys in your dirty Yankee newspaper.' He spat contemptuously into the street, lips twisted in a sneer. 'Marshal!'

'Then turn about and get gone. This is no longer a shipping town and you men are trespassing under terms of the city ordinances.'

'He's the one who kilt our boys!' a red-faced waddy suddenly howled, and sunlight winked on the barrel of the gun that leapt into his fist.

It began that suddenly. Jim's right shoulder dipped and his draw was swift and clean. He waited the shaved tip of a second until certain the man would shoot, then lined him up and blew him out of his saddle.

Without pause he took five long strides to reach Elder's big horse. He reached up lightning-fast and jerked the man down so violently he lost balance and crashed to ground full length.

Jim rammed his Colt muzzle against the man's head and his voice reached every ear.

'This is as far as it goes!' he shouted. 'You men are in breach of the law and I'm ordering you to clear this street right now before anybody else is killed! Now!'

It almost worked.

The Texans had arrived thirsting for trouble, but the trouble had come to them almost too swiftly. Had they taken first blood it might have been different. Now the stark reality of this situation was one pard sprawled dead in an ever widening pool of blood over by the hitch rail of the general store and Elder down on his bony knees in the dust with the foresight of a gleaming Colt .45 jammed into his ear.

This wasn't how it was meant to be.

Then Kittleson moved. The man had tasted humiliation here before and wouldn't swallow the medicine twice. He ripped spur into horsehide and his mount screamed and leapt forward, careening into both Rand and Elder, slamming the latter onto his back and sending the former spinning, his glittering sixshooter flying from his hand.

In an instant the Texans were flooding forward. Hatless and one-armed, Jim made it to his feet and somehow gained the porch of the general store. He was struggling to reach his second Colt but a red-faced herder had his arms pinned to his sides and he couldn't reach his holster. So he ducked his head and smashed his forehead full into the waddy's face, blood gushing hot and crimson.

In moments the porch was a seething mass of surging figures as men fought to get at him, eager to be the one to take the marshal down.

Jim Rand fought like never before. He knew he was done for but amazingly still felt that kernel of calm inside that had been part of him ever since buckling on Fallon's guns.

Then suddenly he was down with the salt taste of blood in his mouth. But his dropped sixgun lay before him upon the boards – and within reach!

He snatched up the weapon in the same instant that a bearded buckaroo, face contorted in hate, came at him swinging a huge cowhide-handled knife.

The Colt bellowed and the Texan's face exploded as though from within. Next instant something crashed against the back of Rand's head and someone was attempting to tear the weapon from his hand. They were all over him, blotting out the light, yet he still heard and identified the voice that rose above the clamor.

'Get the hell off of that man, you varmints!' Then came the guttural roar of a shotgun and he was being showered in blood. Texan blood.

It was blacksmith Buck Wells who'd come out of the Lucky Cuss with the case-keeper's sawed-off in his brawny hands as Jim Rand vanished under an avalanche of cowboys.

The man Wells blew clear off his horse was Sam Kittleson, now sprawled on the ground before the Civil War statue with his left arm blown away. Running in circles, his dog made chilling, whimpering noises around the twitching body.

Wells was forced to trigger again as a bunch of

men came rushing at him across the street, and as two went down under the fearsome blast, Hud Morrow jumped off the gallery to send a big Texan reeling with a blow from a heavy chair-leg.

Bloodied and dazed, Jim struggled to his feet and kicked two attackers aside in time to see the miracle unfold before his eyes.

Wells and Morrow were no longer alone. Far from it. From the emporium now came clerks and counter hands and Ban the Herds marchers brandishing guns and clubs to attack the enemy from the rear, while over by the Plains City's hitch rail several of Rhea's staff were disarming brawlers by the hotel at gunpoint.

A sixgun stabbed a red finger of death and another towner fell. Instantly a rifle cracked from the stage depot landing and a bow-legged Texan threw up his gun and crashed bleeding across Jimson's horse trough, the water instantly turning crimson.

Caught in the cyclone eye of the unfolding chaos, dazed and bloodied with the Colt cocked and ready, Rand squinted through the dust to see Elder, the only man on horseback now, roaring, urging them on.

His Colt bucked against the curve of his hand and Elder pitched from his high saddle screaming with the agony of a smashed knee. Thrusting his gun through his belt, Jim shouldered his way through to the horse and filled the saddle like a trick rider.

Gil Fallon's gun came out again and Jim was laying about him left and right with the long Colt barrel, charging denim-garbed figures down, while all about him was the finest spectacle any lawman could ever see, namely a town fighting for its own survival and honor. Was proud to know that with him or without him wearing the badge, Freetown would now go on to be the kind of place they'd all wanted it to be – Jim Rand, Chain Hollister and Gil Fallon.

It had all begun with Fallon and today would be his legacy . . . .

He shot a man's legs from beneath him – and as the fellow hit ground it was all over. As suddenly as it had begun it was finished with the junction littered by hurt and bloodied figures in denim and leather, beaten men encircled by a vast crowd of righteous, bright-eyed men and women, armoured by their new found courage, looking to their marshal as they had done here before.

Jim triggered into the dusty sky and the silence fell like a cloak.

'Get your dead and injured and get gone,' he said, the big ugly horse dancing beneath him – the enemy's horse. 'You rode in and you'll walk out and you won't come back. Do you know why?'

Dumb, pain-twisted faces stared up at him uncomprehendingly.

He housed Fallon's gun, contemptuous of them now. 'Because I am the law!'

Stiffly he swung down from the horse to move among the mere handful of heroes who remained at the body-littered battleground that was the junction of Longhorn and Plain. Down River Road the tattered enemy was limping across the bridge and out of their lives, harried on their way by the citizens' army.

It was all over at last – really over. You could see it, smell it, feel it as people clustered round him, talking to him, trying to help. He looked like hell, but didn't need any help right now, had nothing to say. His heart was too full as he limped off past the wreckage of a wagon, picked his way through discarded bottles, broken furniture and discarded guns, didn't pause until he stood directly below the balcony of the hotel.

Rhea Tillingham stood on her balcony gazing down. She wore a long brown skirt and severe shirt-waist, her black hair tied back in a bun. She held a smoking carbine pointed at the sky as she stared directly down at him. He half-expected to see outrage, scorn and dismay at what he had unleashed here. Instead the woman smiled proudly, and suddenly, finally it was all clear to him, the mystery solved.

This formidable woman always feared Fallon had died for no good reason, yet had stayed on here in the desperate hope that she might be proved wrong.

That day had come and there was a peace about her now such as he'd never seen before.

As her current escort appeared at her side to take the carbine from her hands, Rhea blew Rand a kiss and gazed down at him as though passing on to him something precious from a man who, at least for as long as they both lived, would always be the immortal marshal.

He saluted and limped on. They were big shoes he was trying to fill. But somehow today they felt just about the right size.